W9-BUV-126

LOVE'S
paradise

LOVE'S *paradise*

CELESTE O. NORFLEET

ARABESQUE®

If you purchased this book without a cover you should be aware
that this book is stolen property. It was reported as "unsold and
destroyed" to the publisher, and neither the author nor the
publisher has received any payment for this "stripped book."

Recycling programs
for this product may
not exist in your area.

LOVE'S PARADISE

ISBN-13: 978-0-373-53453-1

Copyright © 2011 by Celeste O. Norfleet

All rights reserved. The reproduction, transmission or utilization
of this work in whole or in part in any form by any electronic, mechanical
or other means, now known or hereafter invented, including xerography,
photocopying and recording, or in any information storage or retrieval
system, is forbidden without written permission. For permission please
contact Kimani Press, 225 Duncan Mill Road, Toronto, Ontario M3B 3K9,
Canada.

This is a work of fiction. Names, characters, places and incidents are
either the product of the author's imagination or are used fictitiously,
and any resemblance to actual persons, living or dead, business
establishments, events or locales is entirely coincidental.

® and TM are trademarks. Trademarks indicated with ® are registered in
the United States Patent and Trademark Office, the Canadian Trade Marks
Office and/or other countries.

www.kimanipress.com

Printed in U.S.A.

Dear Reader,

I introduced Louise "Mamma Lou" Gates in my first romance novel, *Priceless Gift,* in 2002. Since then I have written eight more novels in the series—including this one, *A Christmas Wish, One Sure Thing, Irresistible You, The Fine Art of Love, Following Love, When Love Calls* and *Love Me Now*— featuring the gregarious octogenarian. *Love's Paradise* is the latest book in the Mamma Lou series, and takes place on Crescent Island. Over the years, readers have asked me to revisit the island. So this story takes you back to where it all began.

In *Love's Paradise,* I introduce Sheri Summers, a historian, and reintroduce Jordan Hamilton, an architect turned developer, who is also one of the Hamilton brothers from *Following Love.* Although they are on opposite sides of a contentious dispute, the two find it impossible to walk away from their feelings a second time.

Look for more Mamma Lou novels soon.

Enjoy!

Celeste O. Norfleet

www.celesteonorfleet.wordpress.com

Matchmaker Series Family Tree

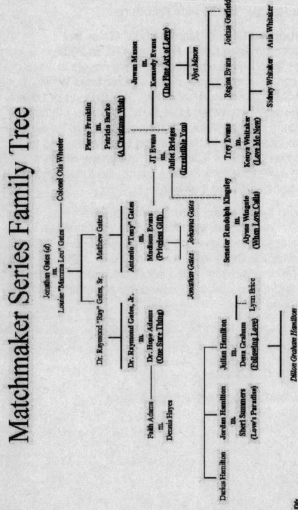

Jonathan Gates (d)
m.
Louise "Mamma Lou" Gates ——— Colonel Otis Wheeler

Dr. Raymond "Ray" Gates, Jr.
m.
Dr. Hope Adams
(One Sure Thing)

Matthew Gates

Antonio "Tony" Gates
Madison Evans
(Priceless Gift)

Pierce Franklin
m.
Patricia Burke
(A Christmas Wish)

Jinvan Mason
m.
Kennedy Evans
(The Blue Art of Love)

JT Evans
m.
Juliet Bridges
(Irresistible You)

Senator Randolph Kingsley
m.
Alyssa Wingate
(When Love Calls)

Johanna Gates

Jonathan Gates

Nya Mason

Trey Evans
m.
Keeya Whitaker
(Love Me Now)

Regina Evans   Joshua Garfield

Sidney Whitaker   Asia Whitaker

Faith Adams
m.
Dennis Hayes

Julian Hamilton
m.
Dena Graham
(Following Love)

Lynn Brice

Jordan Hamilton
Sheri Summers
(Love's Paradise)

Darius Hamilton

Dillon Graham Hamilton

Indic - Edit

To Fate & Fortune

Prologue

Fall carnival, Crescent Island, Virginia
October 1947

"Oh, Louise, have you ever seen anything so amazing?" Emma sighed contentedly as she and her sister walked arm in arm through the Crescent Island fairgrounds. "What do they call this island again?"

"God's garden," Louise said.

"Yes, that's it. It's simply the most beautiful place in the world to go just to get away from everything."

"Em, you say that about every place we go."

"I do not," Emma protested and then just as quickly relented. "Okay, maybe I do. But I really mean it this time. Crescent Island is like something out of a fairy tale. It's magical. It's so much better than Ocean City and Cape May where Mom and Dad always want to go. What do you think?"

"I like it. It's nice," Louise said dispassionately.

"Nice! Nice! For heaven's sake, Louise, how can you say that? It's more than just nice! It's…" Emma nudged her sister. "Look, Louise, there he is again," she whispered.

"There who is again?" Louise asked, turning around.

"No, don't turn around. It's that guy I saw earlier. I noticed him looking at you when we were over by the Ferris wheel. I think he's following us."

"It's a carnival, Emma, everybody's following everybody."

"I suppose," Emma said slowly, "but still…"

"Em, you read entirely too many of those detective novels."

"I do not. And I know when someone is following us and he was definitely following us." She looked around, but he had suddenly vanished. "Uhummm, I wonder where he went," she said.

"What do you want to do next?" Louise asked.

"I have an idea. Why don't we get our fortunes told? Carnivals like this always have fortune-tellers, right?"

"Emma, I am not sitting still just to have someone look at my palm and tell me what I already know. I'm too sensible for that and you should be, too. I'm a practical woman. So why on earth would I believe a fortune-teller who's going to tell me what I already know?"

"For fun, of course," Emma said quickly, then glanced over her sister's shoulder. "Look, there's a tent over there. It says fortune-teller. Come on, Louise, let's do it."

"I think I'll pass. But you go ahead and have fun. I'll wait here."

"No, you have to come, too. It'll be fun."

"No."

"Louise Simmons, where is your sense of adventure?" she said as she linked her arm with her sister's and headed toward the tent. Moments later they stood at the entrance. Emma looked up at the handwritten sign that read, Madam Camille, Fortune-teller.

Come on," she whispered as she disappeared into the tent. Louise sighed loudly and followed.

The inside of the tent was everything Louise had expected. The place was dimly lit yet quite colorful. There were candles all around and ornate-looking tapestries covering the walls that surrounded a table in the center of the room. A young woman, just a few years older than Louise, sat smiling as she shuffled a deck of tarot cards while watching them. She moved the large crystal ball to the side and spread the cards out across the table.

She was slight and willowy with a soft, whispery voice that immediately made you draw nearer to hear her words. She had a thicket of black hair piled up in a mass of curls on top of her head. She wore a dark colored print dress with a white lace collar. She was barefoot, but had a pair of high heels set neatly to the side. Her eyes were light green and piercing. "I've been waiting for you. Welcome. Who wants to go first?"

Emma smiled brightly. "Me first."

Louise nodded and stepped back outside the tent. Ten minutes later Emma emerged smiling from ear to ear. "She's amazing," she whispered in awe. "She told me about my life and about my future. I'm going to be an artist just like I've always dreamed. I'm so happy. Go ahead, it's your turn."

Despite her reservations, curiosity got the best of her and Louise decided to get her fortune read. She ducked inside the tent and looked around, expecting to see the crystal ball in the center of the table again. But it was gone. "I guess it's my turn," she said, as she walked toward the cushioned chair and sat down across the table from the fortune-teller.

"I take it you're not a believer."

"Did the crystal ball tell you that?" Louise said sarcastically.

The young woman glanced at the large, glass

ball on the chair beside her. "Actually I only use that to check my lipstick. So no, I don't need a crystal ball, runes or tarot cards to read the expression on your face. No matter. Sit and give me your hands."

"No tea leaves?"

"I prefer coffee," she said, gesturing for Louise to hold out her hands.

Louise smiled. Apparently Madame Camille had a sense of humor. "Okay, I'll give it a try," she said. She extended her hands—palms side up.

"I don't read palms, either," the fortune-teller said. "I sense things about people when I touch them," Madame Camille said, holding Louise's hands. "You're not very easy to read. No surprise there. But I do see that you have a very special gift."

"What kind of gift?" Louise asked.

Madame Camille didn't answer but instead continued to hold Louise's hand. She took a deep breath then bowed her head and closed her eyes to concentrate a bit more. A few seconds later she opened her eyes and looked up. "This won't do for you. You're too strong-willed."

Louise nodded smugly then got up to leave.

"No, wait. Sit. Stay. There's more."

Louise sat back down and watched as Madame Camille slowly shuffled the deck of large over-size cards. They were unwieldy, worn and tattered around the edges. Still she shuffled them then stacked the deck in front of Louise, motioning for her to cut the deck. She did.

Madame Camille arrayed the cards on the table faceup, aligning each one precisely. She leaned in and nodded her head, smiling. "Do you have a question?" she asked.

"Yes, will I ever know true love?"

"You already do. But your heart is empty right now. It'll soon be filled. A new love is at the gates. Be open to him when he comes."

"I don't understand."

"There was true love in your life for a short time. He's gone now, but he will return later. But for now…"

"When, when will he return?" Louise asked impatiently.

Madame Camille shook her head. "Not for a very, very long time. But for now, know that there is a new love on the horizon. He's waiting for you right now. Your heart's emptiness will soon be filled. That's all I can tell you."

Louise paid the fortune-teller then stood to leave. As she began to turn away she noticed that Madame Camille was staring up at her. "What gift?" Louise asked.

The fortune-teller nodded. "I knew you'd ask. You see the spark of love in others. Your gift is to show them the way." Louise nodded and left. When she was outside the tent, she saw Emma smiling broadly.

"How'd it go?" Emma asked excitedly. "No, don't tell me or it won't come true."

They began walking toward the carousel. They stepped up and sat on one of the benches as young children around them scurried to climb onto the horses.

"There he is again. He's back and he's still looking at you." Louise turned around slowly. A young man stood by the railing looking at her. "He's really handsome, too," Emma said dreamily as she openly stared at him each time they circled past him. "Told you he was looking at you," she said.

He smiled and nodded slightly. Louise returned the gesture.

Spinning slowly as music played, the carousel continued round and round. Louise licked her lips and steadied her nerves as they circled out of his view. She sighed and finally released the breath she hadn't even realized she'd been holding.

"Do you know him?" Emma whispered excitedly as the carousel rotated away from him.

"No. Believe me, I'd remember him. Maybe he's not looking at me," Louise said, turning her head to look behind her to confirm that she and her sister were the only two in his line of vision. "He might have just been glancing in this direction."

"If you think that, then you need your eyes examined."

The carousel spun at a steady rate as Louise's heart raced each time it circled around. Her eyes connected with his again and again. He was smiling now. She smiled back. The next time around she decided to wave, but there was no next time. He was gone. After a while the ride began to slow until it reached a complete stop. Louise and Emma stood to get off. She glanced around curiously, but saw her admirer was nowhere in sight. "Are you okay?" Emma asked.

"Yes, I'm fine."

"Disappointed," Emma added.

"About what?" Louise said lightly.

"Him not being here," she said.

"Not at all," Louise lied as she glanced around nonchalantly one last time. "It's time I stop mooning over guys who are not even here. I've decided. I'm turning over a new leaf. This is the new me and it starts right now." She turned and stopped short. He was standing behind her holding a bag of popcorn, a soda and some cotton candy.

"Hi," he said, smiling. "I got these for you and your friend. My name is Jonathan Gates."

Chapter 1

Present day

The Hamilton Development construction site was located on the southwest shore of Crescent Island. The site was busy as usual. Six months into an eight-month project, the final stages of construction were almost complete. Still, staying on schedule was important. The main building, situated on fifteen acres of land, was a breathtakingly restored nineteenth-century farmhouse manor. Once it was completed, it would be the most impressive corporate resort on the island, and the crowning achievement of the development company. As the main site neared completion, workers were beginning to turn their attention to a secondary site.

Two men stood over a deep hole as a third man pulled a thick rubber hose out of the murky pit of water. He turned and waved. "Okay, turn it off," he yelled. A fourth man flipped a switch and the sound of the generator slowed to a halt. Water trickled from the end of the hose into the hole.

"There, see, look. I told you something was sticking out of the ground down there. It looks like some pieces of wood."

"Yeah, all right, I see it." The foreman got down on his knees, extended his arm and tried to pull out a bowed piece of wood, but couldn't. "It's buried too far down to pull it out."

"We've got to excavate this area and make it level. Skip the pump, get the backhoe up here. And clear that other stuff out of there. Let's get this done before we leave here today."

Moments later a large backhoe ambled up along the side of the area and parked beside the hole. The steel shovel gouged into the earth, dislodging sludge, soil and scattered debris. The shovel shifted to the side and dumped the contents and then plunged back into the hole a second and third time. The fourth time there was a loud scraping sound and the equipment shut off completely. Everybody stood back. "What the hell is that?" the operator said as he cut the engine, leaning out of the cab.

"Sounds like you just hit something." The men looked down to see sludge and slats of wood protruding from the hole. There was a bottle floating in the sludge. One of crew grabbed the bottle, wiped the sludge away then tossed it to the side with the other debris. Another worker walked over and picked it up. "Yo, I'm gonna keep this," he said. "My girlfriend is gonna love it. She collects old things like this."

"Nah, it doesn't work like that on this construction site, dude. Whatever we find goes to the office. No exceptions."

"Yo, man, it's just an old medicine bottle. No big deal."

"No exceptions. Losing your job isn't worth a souvenir, is it?"

The worker grudgingly tossed the bottle to the side with the other debris. Then the man in the cab tried to start up the backhoe again. It made a grinding sound then sputtered and stopped again. "Damn, I think the crane's jammed. It sounds like there's something wrong with the hydraulics."

"Whoa, check it out. That's a lot of wood sticking out on the side down there."

"No big deal, it's just some wood."

"I don't think so, call somebody up here."

One of the crewmen standing around pulled out

his cell phone and called the on-site manager. "Yo, Ian. We need you up here at the secondary site, man."

A few minutes later Ian Parker approached the site. He looked down in the hole and then at the broken backhoe. He shook his head in frustration. It was going to be one of those days.

Sheri Summers was feeling restless and impatient and it was driving her nuts. She glanced at her watch. It had been three hours since the conversation that had started it all. She was still seething. Her boss Jack McDonald's final assessment of her job performance was clear. He thought she didn't have what it took. She could still hear his words echoing in her ears. *You need to have passion to do this job. You don't have that. Besides, we need you back here in D.C. sooner rather than later.*

Was he kidding? She had more passion for her work in her pinkie finger than most people had in their entire body. Yeah, she was furious. He couldn't be more wrong about her. And given the opportunity, she intended to make him eat his words.

Sheri turned and looked out the window. It was the beginning of fall, her favorite time of year. She suddenly felt the temptation to go out and do something wild, something rash. It was a sense of restlessness and anxiousness that she always felt around this time of year. Her grandmother Camille, a fortune-teller, called it her psychic nature coming to life. She didn't know about all that. All she knew was that she had a feeling that something was in the wind, she just didn't know what it was.

She was counting the days until she would have to leave, and time was not on her side. She took a deep breath and felt the energy around her. Everything she knew and loved was coming to an end. Distracted, she closed the book she'd been only half reading and pushed it aside. She stood and walked over to the large dormer window in the attic and looked out at the view.

The tourist season was almost over, yet there were still some vacationers lingering on the island, enjoying the last days of Indian summer. The leaves on the trees hadn't turned colors yet. But the October wind seemed to creep through the drafty old building, sending an imaginary chill through her body. Although it was unseasonably warm outside, inside it seemed much colder. Sheri wrapped her arms around her body, knowing it wasn't the weather that had raised prickly goose bumps on her skin.

The attic was on the fourth floor of the Crescent Island Museum, which was at the far end of town. The museum, a popular tourist attraction, was perched high on a hill, overlooking the city like a guardian angel. From her vantage point, she could see Main Street, the main ferry station and several boutiques and souvenir shops, some of which had been there for well over a century. She reflected on what she liked to call the margins of history.

A deep sense of pride filled her. This was her hometown. Crescent Island was steeped in culture and tradition. Its past was the foundation for what she hoped would be a promising career as a historian. The island's charm, warmth and hospitality were well-known, drawing visitors from across the country. It was also becoming the summer destination for Washingtonians and those looking for a break from the hustle and bustle of the Hamptons and Martha's Vineyard.

This is where she'd grown up. But soon those memories—that history—would no longer be relevant. All her life she'd heard stories about the island's rich history from her grandmother. And as the museum's resident historian and research coordinator, she took pride in preserving its past. Still, the idea of change weighed heavily on her. Her grandmother would say it was foreshadowing a new life. But she was a pragmatist by nature and didn't believe in all that fortune-telling mumbo jumbo. All she knew was that change was in the air and not necessarily for the better.

To ease her restlessness, she settled back into one of the old, uncomfortable chairs that was in the corner of her makeshift museum office. She pulled another book from the stack of dozens that were piled high around her. She had to focus and not let the feeling of melancholy affect her.

She heard her cell phone vibrate. She looked over at the device sitting on the tabletop. She wasn't in the mood to talk, so she picked up the phone to check the caller ID since she'd been screening her calls all afternoon. Looking at the number, she closed her eyes and shook her head, knowing she had to get this over with so she might as well do it now. "Hi, Mom," she said.

"Hi, Sweets. I just got a phone call from Mamma Lou. She wanted to make sure we were attending her gathering Friday night. Are you still going?"

"Yes, I'll be there. No problem, as long as there's not some guy she's set me up with waiting for me with a wedding ring in his pocket."

"What are you talking about?"

"Mamma Lou and her matchmaking," she said. Her mother chuckled. "It's not funny. I'm starting to get paranoid about it. Every time I see her, I'm afraid someone is gonna jump out and propose to me on the spot."

Lois laughed this time. "Come on, Sweets, you're being unreasonable. Besides, do you know how many women would love to have Mamma Lou find them a mate?"

"Well, not me. She tried to set me up with a guy about a year ago. He was totally wrong for me and he was a jerk. He spent the whole date looking at other women."

"Well, knowing Mamma Lou it's highly possible that she's got somebody in mind for you. But I think she's been too busy with the foundation to play matchmaker Friday evening."

"I hope so. I'm not in the mood for more drama."

"More drama? That doesn't sound good. What happened? How did your review go with your boss this morning?"

"Not well," Sheri said.

"What do you mean not well? What did he say?"

"Jack's transferring me back to D.C. He said that I'm overqualified to be curator of the museum and that my enthusiasm was mediocre at best. And I lacked the kind of bold vision and initiative needed for the job. His exact words were, 'You need to have passion to do this job.' According to him, he just hasn't seen it and they need me back in D.C as soon as possible."

"Oh, that's ridiculous. The man is obviously an idiot. He wouldn't know talent if it jumped up and bit him. This is about being a curator in a small museum, not brain surgery. Of course you have passion! Anyone with half a brain can see that you're passionate about your work. What's wrong with him?" Lois Chambers said testily.

Sheri's mother had always been her daughter's champion and a constant source of support for her children. She was loving and nurturing, and also smart and savvy. So it was no surprise that she ran the most popular and successful bed-and-breakfast inn on the island. "You're an exceptional scholar and historian. And you're brilliant at your job. Crescent Island Museum would be damn lucky to have you as its full-time curator. If he can't see that then he's a bigger jacka—"

"Mom, it's okay, really. I tried. That's all I can do and I did my best. When my tenure here is up next month, I'll just go back to the Smithsonian Institution."

"Sheri, you can do battle with the best of them. I've seen you with your brothers for heaven's sake. When you want something, you're tenacious. Fight for this if you really want it."

Her mother was right. She could stand toe-to-toe and do battle with anyone. And given the opportunity, she was going to prove it. "…when you follow what's in your heart, you are unstoppable," her mother said. "I've seen it too many times…."

"Sheri. Sheri, where are you?"

Sheri looked up as her assistant, Eugenia Hopkins, called out her name. "Mom, I gotta go. I'll pick up Grandma tonight and call you later. Bye." She ended the call.

"Yeah, I'm up here," Sheri yelled. It was almost closing time and most of the exhibits and galleries were located on the first and second floors, so she knew no one would probably hear them.

"Sheri!"

"In here, in the archive area," Sheri said, not quite as loudly this time, since her assistant was on the top floor now.

Eugenia—Genie, to all of her friends—came barreling down the hall to the doorway. Breathlessly, she smiled as she leaned back against the door frame to catch her breath. "Oh, my God, there you are. I just ran up all those stairs," she said, and then paused. "I've been looking everywhere for you. I called your office phone a dozen times on the way over here."

"I've been up here in the archives most of the morning gathering books for the upcoming exhibition. What's going on?"

"No, no, no, forget all that."

"Wait, Genie, what are you doing here? You're not scheduled to work today. Don't you have classes this afternoon?"

"Yeah, but this is way more important. You are never going to believe what's going on—" She paused, held her hand to her chest to catch her breath again. "The text message I just got. I can hardly believe it myself." She hurried across the open space.

"What are you talking about? What's going on?" Sheri stood and came around to the front of the table. She knew Genie well enough to realize that she was at times overly excitable. The smallest finding in a newspaper or online sent her into orbit for weeks, so seeing her enthusiasm now wasn't unusual. She was still in college majoring in history and had been Sheri's intern during the summer. Now she worked in the museum gift shop and was also an unpaid part-time assistant, spending most of her time in the library and the archives, sorting artifacts and filing data electronically. Genie hoped to one day work at the Smithsonian as a curator.

"I've been trying to contact you for the past fifteen minutes. We've gotta go now," Genie continued excitedly.

Sheri panicked. "Go where? Is there something wrong in the museum? Another fire?"

"No, no, no, nothing like that. It's fine. Everything's okay in the museum. But listen, I just got a text message from my boyfriend, Jamie. He sent a picture he took at his job. He works at that big construction site at Crescent Point. They just found something at the site."

Sheri's heart tumbled. She knew Crescent Point and she knew about the development being built there. She looked at her assistant sternly. "What do you mean they just found something? Who found something at that site?"

"Look, see…" Genie said, giving Sheri her cell phone.

Sheri took the phone and looked at the down-loaded picture. It was an image of an old medi-cine bottle. She squinted, noting the shape and size. It was unusual by modern-day standards, but certainly nothing to get excited about. Then she pressed the screen for the next photo, shrugged and shook her head. "It's a pile of trash and an old bottle. I don't get it."

"Now keep going. Check out the next photos."

Sheri moved to the next photo. It was a close-up and a much clearer shot. There was a large hole, half filled with dirty water with something pro-truding out of it. "It looks like the bottom edge of an old bucket with the letters *e-n-t* on the side." She clicked to the next photo, which was an even better close-up of the hole. "I still don't get it."

"Keep going, look at the next one," Genie in-sisted.

There was less water in the hole and what she thought was a bucket was actually thicker, rounder and more defined. She tilted her head then turned the phone upside down. The image looked differ-ent. There were also more letters, *c-e-n-t*. "Wait, what? That's not a bucket." She quickly forwarded to the next photo. It was a picture of Genie and her boyfriend waving and smiling at the beach. She went back to the last photo. She studied it again. Half smiling, she couldn't believe her eyes. She looked up at Genie, who was standing next to her the whole time. "It looks like the outline of a bell, a ship's bell. Wait, this can't be what I think it is?"

Genie nodded gleefully. "The *Crescent* bell," she squealed excitedly, and then started giggling wildly. Sheri clicked back to the first few photos and stopped at the one with the close-up of the side of the bell. "Oh, my God, I can't believe it," she said. "My boyfriend actually found the wreckage of the *Crescent* ship? I can't wait to tell everybody I know. I'm going on Facebook and Twitter right now. We're gonna be famous."

"Genie, Genie, calm down. At this point, we don't know what was found. You can't tell anyone about this until it's been confirmed one way or the other. Anything else would be irresponsible."

"But this is it. I just know it," Genie said, emphatically.

"What's that beside the bottle?" Sheri asked, noting the size and shape in comparison to the bottle. "It looks a little like a bugler's mouthpiece," she said.

"They think it's an old golf tee. But if it is what you say it is then it's much better, right?"

"A golf tee?" Sheri said, surprised.

"Yes, see that's why we gotta go. Come on," Genie said, and motioned. "I'll tell you the rest on the way."

Sheri went back to the table, closed the books, grabbed her notebook and laptop and followed

Genie down the hallway then down the steps. "Okay, so how did all this happen?" Sheri asked.

"So, remember all the rain we've been having lately and the really heavy downpour we had last night?" she began, nearly tripping down the steps as she talked.

"Yes, what about it?"

"Well, apparently it eroded the side of this mound of dirt they were beginning to level and flooded a hole that had been dug out a few weeks ago. The work crew started pumping the water out of the hole this morning and they found the bottle floating on top. Jamie took pictures. They just tossed it aside, but my boyfriend remembered seeing something like the bottle here at the museum." Genie's cell phone beeped. Sheri gave the phone back to her, and she immediately began text messaging.

"Granted, it doesn't have to be the *Crescent* or even a ship's bell. An out-of-focus image on a cell phone doesn't prove anything."

"But it could be, right? It could be?" Genie said, as she frantically texted.

Sheri knew exactly what she meant. The discovery, if it was the *Crescent,* would be huge. But she didn't want to speculate. She didn't want to think about the possibility that it could be the legendary ship. "No. There's still not nearly enough evidence to jump to that conclusion," she said as she shook her head. "We need more than an artifact half-covered in mud with letters on it."

Genie looked almost crushed.

"We don't do maybes or what ifs. We need cold, hard, indisputable evidence."

Genie nodded. They continued in silence, knowing what they needed was a miracle. Just then Genie's phone beeped again. There was another text message and downloaded image. She opened it to see what her boyfriend had sent. She smiled and handed her phone to Sheri. "I think we just got cold, hard, indisputable evidence."

Sheri nodded. "Yeah, we need to get to the site right now."

"Definitely," Genie said, racing down the stairs.

"Wait," Sheri said as she trailed Genie. "I need to go back to my office and get my backpack and camera."

"Okay, I'll get my Jeep and meet you out front."

Sheri headed to her office with no idea what she was getting herself into. A sense of trepidation suddenly seized her, quelling some of the excitement. Finding an old medicine bottle and what looked like a ship's bell was promising. But the possibility of unearthing what looked like the ribbed, wooden frame of the ship's hull was definitely an important find. Her heart began to race as she stuffed her laptop in her backpack, grabbed her camera, her jacket and then headed out.

She locked her office door, hurried downstairs through the museum and quickly caught up with Genie just as she drove up to the front entrance. She sidestepped a puddle then looked down at her outfit. She hadn't expected to be outside, away from the museum that day, so she certainly hadn't dressed to dig around a construction site. Four-inch stilettos and a business suit would have to do. As soon as she climbed into the passenger seat, Genie took off. She glanced into the backseat. Genie had brought just about everything from her office. "Okay, Hamilton Development is at Crescent Point. It's on the other side of the island."

"How long has your boyfriend worked for them?" Sheri asked.

"Only a few weeks, he doesn't know much about them, just that he hates working there. He said that Jordan Hamilton is a coldhearted workaholic. And believe me, that's putting it nicely. Apparently Jordan and his foreman complain about everything Jamie does. The thing is Jamie had worked for his father's construction company just about all his life before it went bankrupt. So he thinks he can do the same things he used to. At his father's company, he didn't really do anything. He'd go in late and sleep all day in the trailer. He can't do that here. He actually has to do work and he hates it. Anyway, he said Jordan is the worst of the three brothers."

"There are three brothers?" Sheri asked.

"Sheri, seriously, you must have had your head in the sand these past months."

"Actually running the museum without a curator on a shoestring budget, keeping the building from falling in on our heads, organizing the historical records and putting them in a database has kept me more than a little busy. So yeah, I guess I haven't had time to pay attention to all the new real estate developments and construction on the island."

"Yeah, I guess you're right," said Genie. "So anyway the company is owned by three brothers. All are rich and too gorgeous. Their main office is in Northern Virginia somewhere near D.C., I think. Two of the brothers are single, but one of them just got married."

"Which one?" she asked quickly, hoping not to sound like she had way too much interest for her own good.

"I don't know," Genie said. "So, anyway they're rich. I saw a picture of all three of them at this formal thing in D.C. Ohmygod! They are too gorgeous. They're tall, dark and handsome and built like you wouldn't believe."

Sheri wasn't at all surprised by Genie's wealth of information about their looks and dating habits. When it came to men, she was information central. "Didn't you meet one of them before?" Genie asked.

Sheri took a deep breath. Thinking about their

meeting wasn't something she liked doing. "It was a while ago and it was very brief," she said truthfully.

"Who was it? What was he like?" Genie asked.

"I don't remember," she lied.

"Well, if it was Jordan Hamilton you would have definitely remembered. Jamie said he was the worst of the three. And since they apparently all take turns being on-site, he should know. I'd love to meet him. But it's Monday and he never comes in on Monday."

Sheri purposely didn't respond. Thinking about him would mean remembering their encounter.

"I think Jordan's the bad boy of the three brothers," Genie continued. "You know, the hard-ass who's oh-so-hot." She smiled then stopped at a traffic light and glanced at her cell phone. "Okay, my boyfriend just texted me and said half the water's already out. There's more wood from the hull of the ship showing. Can you believe it? The wooden planks of the hull—it's sounding more and more like a ship to me."

Sheri felt a twinge of excitement begin to creep inside her. There were endless possibilities as to what it actually could be, but the remote chance that it was a hull was just too good to be true. "Okay, we can't get too excited. We're scientists—scholars," Sheri said firmly. "Let's not jump the gun here. We need to examine the site first before we draw any conclusions."

"Yeah, yeah, I know all that. But, can you believe it? It's so exciting. Just imagine. We're right here at the start of something this amazing. I can't wait to excavate."

"We'll have to wait and see. It may not even come to that," Sheri said, dashing Genie's hopes again. She hated doing it, but she needed Genie to be calm and rational.

"I know, but still, can you imagine…?"

Sheri didn't have to imagine, she was already there. Finding the wreckage of the *Crescent* would be extraordinary. No, it would be monumental. It would also validate the research she'd been working on for years.

Genie continued chattering as they drove across the island toward Crescent Point. Sheri was quiet throughout much of the ride. Too many things were on her mind. Fifteen minutes later they pulled into the parking lot. Sheri looked up at the large sign, Hamilton Development Corporation. She shivered. Immediately the hairs on the back of her neck stood on end.

They got out, grabbed their gear and headed to the front gate. A security guard watched them approach. He met them halfway shaking his head and pointing behind them. "I'm sorry, girls, this is a construction site. You gotta leave."

"We'd like to speak to whoever is in charge, please."

"Regarding?" the guard asked.

"We're from the Crescent Island Museum," Sheri began as she showed her ID. "We'd like to speak with someone about items found on this property."

"You're mistaken, there were no items found here."

"I believe there were, so please call whomever you need. We'd like to speak to them," she insisted.

He chuckled while looking deadly serious. "Look, this isn't the place you want to be. So why don't you girls turn your little Jeep around and get yourselves back to the museum. Because you're not getting on this property, that's just not going to happen," he said.

Sheri raised her chin and glared at him. She had no intention of leaving and the man's condescending tone and the fact that he insisted on calling them girls irked her. But what really made her angry was the fact that he was standing in the way of uncovering something of huge historical significance. "Don't patronize us. And we're not girls, so I suggest you get someone down here now!" she said. The tone of her voice was unmistakable. She meant business. He nodded and smiled again as he pulled out his cell phone and made a call. Moments later a woman approached dressed in jeans, a T-shirt, a lightweight jacket with a company logo and carrying a hard hat with her cell phone to her ear. She hung up as soon as she neared them.

"Hi, I'm Tamika Smith, the development's operations assistant. How can I help you?" she said, friendly enough.

"Yes, hi, I hope so. My name is Sheri Summers and this is my assistant, Genie Hopkins." They shook hands. "We're with the Crescent Island Museum and Smithsonian Institution. I believe you found some items this morning that may be of significant historical value."

"Historical value? Here? No, you must be mistaken," she said, self-assuredly.

"I don't think so," Sheri said firmly.

"We're in the process of finalizing this development site. If something had been uncovered, we would have certainly found it months ago and contacted the proper authorities."

"I believe this was found in a new location."

"The secondary site?" she asked with added interest. "Did someone from the site contact you?" Tamika asked.

"In a manner of speaking, yes. Photos were sent to the museum."

"Okay, hold on. Let me check with our on-site manager," she called someone and repeated what Sheri had just told her. She stepped away out of earshot and continued her conversation.

Genie leaned over to Sheri. "I had no idea this

place was so big. It's huge and it looks like they're almost done."

Sheri nodded as she looked around. Genie was right. The site was a lot larger than she'd expected. Of course she knew about the huge construction project. Everybody on the island knew. For a while Hamilton's real estate development had created a huge rift in the community. After a few minutes the woman turned back around to face them.

"Okay, Ian Parker, the on-site manager, will meet you at the office trailers. He's tied up at the moment, but you can wait for him. Follow me."

"Thank you," Sheri said as she and Genie followed her through the entrance to the construction site. Teetering on her high heels, she meandered her way through the puddles and mud around the largest building being constructed on the site, and continued until they reached a paved open space. They were headed toward what looked like oversize trailers parked at the opposite end of the site. As they walked, Sheri looked across at the main building. To her surprise the development was a lot further along than she'd expected. The roof had been completed and the windows had been framed in place. Bricklayers were perched upon scaffolding beside the concrete that formed the outside walls. It appeared that work had begun on the interior, with flooring piled high in front of the building. Tamika led them to a large trailer. As they climbed the steps to the entrance, Tamika knocked and opened the door, ushering them inside.

"Okay, you can wait in here. Ian will be with you as soon as he can."

Sheri and Genie took a seat. They waited and waited, and after thirty-five minutes Sheri's patience was quickly running out, not that she had much to begin with. "This is ridiculous," she said, now that she was beyond being aggravated. "We've been more than patient."

Genie pulled out her cell phone and began texting. "I just texted my boyfriend. He's on his way to show us to the site. He said to just follow him and pretend like we don't know him," she added.

They went outside. A few minutes later Jamie arrived. He walked past them without speaking, not wanting to jeopardize his job. Sheri and Genie followed far enough behind him so as not to raise suspicion. He led them to a remote area of land closer to the beach. There were a few men standing around looking into the engine compartment of a backhoe.

Sheri and Genie walked up to the small incline of dirt. There was a pile of debris, overgrowth and dead wood tossed to the side. They walked over to inspect it more closely. Sheri bent down and examined the small fragment. The wood still showed signs of even cuts resembling floor planks.

"They look like plank fragments, right?" Genie

said over her shoulder. Sheri nodded then stood up. They turned and looked down at the small crater near the backhoe.

It was exactly like the images Genie's boyfriend had sent them. The water was still being suctioned out and what looked like the remnants of a ship's hull were plainly visible along with something else. Genie grabbed Sheri's arm. "Look over there in the hole. There it is. It really is a ship's bell. And there, see, it's upside down. It says *s-c-e-n-t*."

"Yes, that's exactly what it looks like." Sheri smiled. A bubble of excitement swelled inside her. She felt almost giddy. "The inscription on the outside bell is still partially concealed, but..." She bent down to get a better look. "Okay. We need to take pictures and get samples to verify carbon dating and we'll definitely need to examine the bell in a more controlled environment." She pulled out her camera and started taking pictures.

"All right, let's see if we got this thing going now," someone called out behind them. Genie stood and turned around to see what was happening. The three men standing around at the backhoe stepped away. The one man who had been working on the backhoe closed the top of the engine compartment, grabbed his work gloves from his back pocket and put them on. He climbed back up into the cab of the truck.

"Give him some room," one of the men said. Everyone stepped back. "Sheri," Genie began, "I think they're about to…"

Sheri turned. Just then a man sitting in the cab of the huge backhoe started the engine and shifted gears. The giant shovel roared to life and lurched in the direction of the hole. The men standing around stood back anticipating what would happen next. Sheri's heart jumped. She knew, too. "No, no, no, stop!" she called out, stepping in front of the huge machine just as it raised its massive arm. The man driving stopped, cut the engine and jumped out.

"What the hell are you doing? Are you crazy, lady? Somebody, get this woman out of here." Nobody moved.

Genie hurried to Sheri's side. "You can't do this. You might be destroying history," she said.

"Great, now there are two of them. All right, somebody get security out here now. Look ladies, I don't know who you are or why you're here, but this is a work site. You need to leave now."

"We're not going anywhere. Can't you see what you're about to destroy?" Genie protested passionately. "Look, look what you're about to demolish." Everybody looked into the hole at the wet sand, silt and sludge, and the rotted wooden planks.

"Ladies, whoever you are…"

"We're from the Crescent Island Museum representing the Smithsonian Institution. You need to stop what you're doing right now and I need to speak to someone in authority."

"Lady, there's only one person who tells me to stop digging and he's not here."

"Fine, who is he," she said.

"Jordan Hamilton," Genie's boyfriend said, walking up to the small gathering of workers. Seeing and hearing him, Genie smiled proudly.

"I'd like to speak with him," Sheri said.

"He's not here," someone in the crowd said.

"He's a busy man, he doesn't come in on Mondays," the man at the backhoe began.

"And I'm a busy woman," Sheri said, directing her attention back to the man sitting at the machine controls. "If he's not here get someone else."

"Lady, look, whatever's down there, I'm digging it up and right now you're in the way of me doing my job. That means you need to move, now!" He climbed into the carriage of the backhoe. She didn't move. He glared at her and waited. Then, seeing that she had no intention of moving, he nodded to one of the men standing around. "Get somebody out here now."

Chapter 2

Jordan Hamilton's perfectly ordered life had been upset. Everything was going wrong today. He parked at the far end of the lot, got out of his truck and slammed the driver's-side door so hard the glass shook. He barely glanced back to see if it had shattered. If it had, he really didn't care one way or the other. He'd had enough of this place and the people. Usually good-humored by nature, he seldom let anything stress him out. But that was before. Now, for some reason, this job had turned into a quagmire and every little thing was a major hassle. Add to that, the clock was ticking on the project. His deadline was tight. He was running out of time, and running out of patience even more quickly.

This was another wasted trip. He walked around to the passenger's side, grabbed the tube of blueprints and his briefcase off the seat and slammed the passenger door, too. He was furious. He'd spent the morning going head-to-head with Nolan Chambers, the chairman of the supervisory committee and dealing with inane questions, ludicrous suggestions and absurd requests. All of it added up to another wasted day.

That was the part of the job he despised. His brothers, Julian and Darius, were far better at the politicking thing than he was, and they both had the kind of people skills—the knack for schmoozing—that he didn't. Either way, this definitely wasn't what he needed to do right now. He'd been dodging, sidestepping and trying to avoid nearly impossible obstacles since he'd been working on the project.

After a two-month delay and a number of unforeseen work stoppages, he'd finally gotten the permits and cleared inspections and final approvals he needed to move on to the next phase. The project was still two weeks behind, and if weather began to change, he'd have to halt work again. And he couldn't afford that. Bottom line, this job was costing a fortune and it had turned into a nightmare.

Ultimately he was working against time, and

every day the project was delayed cost him more money. He didn't need unnecessary distractions. More importantly, he'd had enough dealing with the city council and all its rules and regulations. They were wasting his time. He needed to be on site overseeing construction when he was on the island and not babysitting and pandering to know-nothing politicians.

He took a deep breath and released it slowly, knowing he needed to calm down. Aggravation and distractions were how on-site accidents happened. He'd already had one; he didn't need another. He needed to get his focus back on the job. He looked around. It was a gorgeous day. After the past few days of rain, it was good to see the sun shining. At least that was in his favor, he thought. He wasn't sure how many days like this he'd have left.

Jordan pulled out his cell phone to check his messages and then realized it was still turned off from the city council meeting in town earlier. He turned it back on and saw that he'd missed several calls and messages including two from his brothers and one from the on-site manager, Ian Parker.

He called his brothers. Both calls went directly to voice mail. He started walking toward the main entrance of the Hamilton Development site. As soon as he neared the gate he saw that Cleveland, head of site security, usually stationed at the entrance at all times, wasn't there. He had been brought over from the main office because he was loyal and never shirked his responsibilities. There was no way he'd just up and leave his post without a good reason.

As he walked he checked the rest of his phone messages. There were several calls and email messages from vendors and suppliers, including the landscaper he'd been playing phone tag with for the past three days. "Damn," he muttered under his breath as he realized he'd missed the one call he'd been expecting. He called Ian on his cell phone's walkie-talkie feature as he headed to the trailer.

"Yo." Ian's voice came through loud and clear.

"I'm on-site," Jordan said.

"On a Monday?" Ian asked.

"Yeah, I had to be at a Crescent Island City Council meeting this morning."

Ian chuckled knowing Jordan hated dealing with politicians. "How'd that go?" he asked, knowing the answer.

"Exactly as I expected, it was a huge waste of my time," Jordan said.

Ian chuckled again. "Yeah, well, like you said, you expected as much. Still you had to go. You're the face of Hamilton Development here on the island and that means playing nice with the local politicians."

"Actually what it means is another wasted day

and wasting more of my time," he said as he loosened his tie and then waved at a passing worker.

"Well, it could have been worse."

"How's that," Jordan asked.

"You could still be there," Ian said, chuckling.

Jordan smiled and shook his head. "Yeah, right," he said sarcastically. "Actually, I doubt they'll be asking to see me anytime soon."

"Why's that?" Ian asked.

"Let's just say we had an exhaustive discussion on my time management and the cost effectiveness of my having to constantly meet with them."

"You spoke your mind," Ian surmised.

"I made a few things perfectly clear."

"How'd that go over?"

"As expected, but one good thing is I managed to get them to bump up final approval to start the next phase. They're going to review the proposal next week."

"Now that is good news," Ian said.

"Yeah, it should cut a few weeks off the back end. We might just be able to bring this project in on time," Jordan said, not sounding as confident as he should.

"That'll work. I don't see a problem."

"Unfortunately, I missed the landscaper's call earlier."

"Yeah, I know. They called me when they couldn't reach you in the office or on your cell.

I told them what we talked about yesterday. They don't have a problem with it as long as the weather holds out and we don't fall too far behind."

"Good, thanks. Where are you now?" Jordan asked.

"I'm on the third floor of the main building. I just finished triple-checking the electrical wiring. The inspectors just left."

"How'd we do?"

"We're good to go. Everything looks good, no problems. I'm headed down with the paperwork now."

"Okay, I'll meet you at the trailer in a few minutes. I gotta get out of this suit and into some real clothes," he said as he walked across the main grounds to the row of trailers.

"Heads up, we have visitors on site."

"What visitors?" Jordan asked cautiously. "Tamika didn't tell me we were having visitors today."

"I believe they were unplanned. Tamika told me that two women from the local museum are here. They're waiting at the trailer."

"What do they want? A donation or something?" he asked.

"Don't know."

"All right, I'll deal with it," Jordan said just as he stepped out onto the wooden deck outside the trailer. He stopped and looked around at the activity on the work site surrounding him. This was his element. Construction was in his blood. He looked up at the main structure. Although it was not nearly complete, the building was certainly taking shape.

What was once a run-down hotel was now well on its way to becoming a profitable corporate resort. He nodded his approval as he looked at the facade of bricks that covered the face of the structure. Seeing his creation come to fruition always gave him a feeling of accomplishment. He looked up at the sun then back down again, appreciating the way the beam of sunlight played across the building exterior. The rays of sunlight twinkled as they bounced off the building's large glass windows, a detail that had been part of his design, which was meant to be carefully integrated into its natural setting. In Jordan's mind he imagined the finished structure, and it was perfection.

This was why he became an architect. After spending several years with a Los Angeles architectural firm and now working with his brothers, he had honed his design skills to perfection. Each building he worked on had its own unique appeal. Some were simple structures, while others were massive edifices designed to take your breath away. But this one was different. This was the Hamilton brothers' project from beginning to end. He and Julian had scouted locations. Darius had purchased the land and gotten the financing. But it was Jordan who was in charge and bringing their vision to life.

Several workers waved as he passed by. Jordan returned the friendly greetings. These were the men and women he related to best. They worked with their hands and created something out of nothing. He arrived at the trailer and went inside. He looked around. There was no one there. Apparently the visitors had decided to leave. He dropped his brief-case on the desk then went to the large drawing table and pulled the rolled-up plans from the tube. He spread them out and looked them over for the thousandth time. He knew where every brick, pane of glass and screw would be set. He was proud of this building and knew this was only the begin-ning. What started out as a small hotel turned into a resort and then finally into the Hamilton Resort Complex.

He changed his clothes in his private room in the back of the trailer and then returned to the draw-ing table. As soon as he pulled out the blueprints for the electrical, his cell phone rang. He looked at the caller ID then picked up. "Hello, Mrs. Gates," he said cordially.

"Hello, Jordan, now you've been here on Cres-cent Island for months. I think it's high time you call me Mamma Lou, don't you? Your brothers do, everybody else does, and I insist."

"Of course, Mamma Lou, what can I do for you?"

"That's better. Now, I'm just calling to remind you of the small gathering up at the house this weekend for the Gates Heritage Foundation. Remember, it's very informal, nothing big and fancy. It's just members of the foundation and of course my very close friend, Camille Rantone. She's an incredible storyteller and folklorist and definitely someone you should know. And since you're here on Crescent Island all by yourself, I thought you might like to join us. I can promise you some good home cooking and a very entertaining evening."

Jordan smiled. He knew a setup when he heard one and he knew exactly what she was doing. She was setting him up again. It was obvious. He had no idea how his brother Julian had fallen for her matchmaking so easily. She was so obvious. It was the same thing she'd been up to since they'd met at his nephew's birthday party almost a year ago. Thanks to his brother and sister-in-law, Julian and Dena, he knew all about Louise Gates. She was apparently well-known for her matchmaking. He had no intention of walking into one of her matchmaking traps.

"Thank you for the invitation, Mamma Lou, but I'm afraid I'm going to have to pass. My weekends are usually very busy and as you know, I'm very seldom here on the weekends, perhaps another time."

"Of course dear," she said happily. Jordan sighed, certain that he had successfully dodged another of her invitations. "After all, you are a very busy man," she continued, "but then again, so are the others taking the time to attend. That's why there's no set hour to arrive. I thought it would be a lot easier that way. After all it is for charity. So feel free to join us after you're done with your work on Friday. The evening will start at around seven-thirty. Anytime after that will be just fine."

"Actually, Mamma Lou, I always head home on Thursday evenings and don't return to the island until Tuesdays. I'm sure you understand," he said, feeling confident that he'd once again sidestepped any matchmaking plans she might have.

"Well, of course I understand. And I really appreciate you taking the time out of your busy schedule to do this. I'm sure you won't mind coming back to the island Friday evening. After all, it is for charity and you'll have all day Saturday to work. Good, it's settled."

"Mamma Lou…" he began, realizing he'd just been backed into a corner.

"It sounds like you're working entirely too hard. You need some downtime to relax. So, you stop by the manor Friday evening and then get back to your other job on Saturday. So there, see, problem solved. I knew we could work it out. Now if you need a place to stay, you're more than welcome to stay here at the manor anytime. I have plenty of room."

He opened his mouth, and then closed it quickly while shaking his head. She was good, she was very good. "Thank you for the offer, Mamma Lou. I have a condo here that I rent," he began then paused, realizing there was no way he was going to evade her this time. This was his third invitation from Louise Gates and each time he'd successfully avoided her offer. "No promises, but I'll try to make it. Thank you again for the invitation."

"You're very welcome, dear. I look forward to seeing you Friday evening. Have a good day."

"Goodbye, Mamma Lou." He hung up, shaking his head. The woman was impossible. He glanced down at the blueprints and he opened his laptop. Moments later there was an abrupt knock and the door opened. Ian Parker poked his head inside. "Hey, got a minute?"

"Yeah, what's up?" Jordan said as he glanced up then quickly turned back to the plans he'd just started reviewing.

"I got a call from Cleveland, there's…"

Jordan looked up again. "Yeah, I meant to call him. I've had my mind on a dozen things. He wasn't at the gate."

"That's because he's been up at the secondary

site," Ian said, stepping all the way into the trailer. Then he stopped talking and grimaced. "Damn, man, you look like crap."

"Thanks," Jordan said sarcastically as he rubbed the roughness on his chin. He decided to ignore the remark. "So, what's up with Cleveland? Is everything all right?"

"Yeah, he was walking a new guard through the process and then got a call. Apparently our visitors found their way to the secondary site. I think you're gonna need to get up there."

Jordan shook his head. "This day is getting better and better," he grumbled as he grabbed his hard hat and sunglasses and followed Ian out the door. They headed toward the secondary site. He saw several workers gathered around in the distance. "I was just up here late last night and again earlier this morning. It looks like we have some vandalism going on again."

"I'll make sure to file an official report. So, you were up here last night and then again early this morning. Tell me," Ian began, "do you ever sleep at night or do you just roam around the site until dawn? No wonder you look like a zombie."

Jordan chuckled and rubbed the stubble on his chin again. He hadn't shaved today. As a matter of fact he hadn't shaved in the past few days. "Are you gonna get all Dr. Oz on me?"

Ian laughed. "Yeah, it looks like I'm gonna have to."

"Fine, I'll shave. I guess I've just been too busy getting this place up and running."

"See, right there, that's just what I'm talking 'bout. You're letting this project get to you, man. Look at you, you don't have a life outside of this place and now you're starting to micromanage every minute detail. Let it go, man. Take a break. Chill out and relax. Check out some of the local flavor here on the island. Everybody needs some downtime, even you. When's the last time you even went out on a date?"

Jordan didn't reply.

"Uh-huh, that's what I thought. Man, if I didn't know any better, I'd say you were doing that celibacy thing like your brother Julian."

"Nah, man. That's not me."

"Yeah, all right, if you say so," Ian said skeptically. "Still, you need to take some time off and chill."

Jordan knew Ian was right. He was trying to micromanage everything and everyone. It wasn't his style, but this job was too important to him. He didn't want any more unnecessary mistakes. "This island doesn't exactly compare to New York's nightlife. At least not yet," Jordan said.

"No, granted it doesn't." Ian chuckled. "But there are things to do here other than constantly work. I know the company's got a lot of projects going on. But if you burn out, you're no good to anyone. You gotta relax, man. Trust me, this project will get done and if the blueprints and scale models are any indication, it's gonna be majorly impressive. But if you're gonna stress out for the next few months, we're gonna have a serious problem. Why don't you take the weekend off and hang around here? You know it's called God's garden for a reason. This place is like paradise."

"Yeah, it is," he agreed.

"Good, then take advantage of it."

Suddenly suspicious, Jordan looked at Ian. "All right. Did my brothers put you up to this?"

Ian laughed. "Darius and Julian have nothing to do with this. I'm just saying…"

"All right, all right, I get it. Chill out, relax and have some fun. I'll add that to my to-do list. So what's going on up here?" Jordan asked as they neared the site.

"I have no idea," Ian said, squinting against the sun's brightness just as his cell phone rang. He answered and quickly agreed. "It looks like it's just going to be one of those days."

"What's up?" Jordan asked.

"First the backhoe hits something up here on that mound and blows a hydraulic valve and now there's a problem with one of the generators on-site."

"What kind of problem?"

"I don't know. I doubt it's anything serious, but I'm gonna head back and check it out just in case."

"Do you need the electrical plans?"

"Nah."

"All right, I'll see what's going on up here and catch up with you later. Let me know if you need me," Jordan said over his shoulder.

"All right, later," Ian said as he turned and headed back toward the main building. Then he stopped, turned and called out, "Yo, Wilamina just texted you. You need to charge your phone. She just left two messages. Darius needs you to call him."

"Yeah, he's called a few times. I'll get back to him later tonight," he said. Moments later he approached the site. He heard a woman's voice giving what sounded like an extensive lecture on the importance of preserving history. He sighed heavily. After spending the entire morning and most of the afternoon dealing with nonsense, the last thing he needed to do was deal with someone camped out at his work site intent on causing trouble. Several of the men gathered nodded and spoke as he approached. Two men stepped aside as he walked to the front row to listen to the woman's tirade.

Chapter 3

Jordan's first thought was to immediately break this up, get everyone back to work and have Cleveland toss her out. He figured she was just another nutcase rabble-rouser there to cause trouble. They'd had a number of them when the project first started months ago. But seeing her, hearing her, he began to change his mind. She was certainly something to see, dressed in a perfectly tailored business suit and high heels. He smiled. Her passion was almost addictive.

He listened for a few more minutes and couldn't help but be fascinated as he watched this sexy troublemaker have her say. She stood with her back to him, directly in front of his backhoe, preventing the shovel arm from moving. Her fists were planted firmly on her hips. The sight was a bit like David and Goliath, with the backhoe being Goliath. She turned around to make a point. He saw a determined scowl crease her soft brown complexion giving it a fiery red blush. He knew her instantly, but hesitated. She was very different than he remembered.

She was always attractive in a sweet girl-next-door kind of way, but now she was a sultry, hot firecracker and there was something temptingly enticing about her. Maybe it was her passion or her fire—either way he found her exciting. This certainly wasn't the tame, meek woman he'd met months ago.

Her dark, angry brown eyes narrowed and sparkled with enthusiastic zeal as she turned to make yet another point. He watched her mouth as she spoke. She had full, luscious, kissable lips lightly tinted with a soft coral that he doubted had much to do with cosmetics. She had high cheekbones and an elegant face and neck, perfect for the curly hair that barely touched her shoulders. It was obvious she believed in whatever she was talking about. He wondered just how passionate she was about other things. He knew the face and body, but not her name. "Do you know who she is?" he asked a couple of the workers standing beside him.

Both men shook their heads. Then Jamie, standing nearby, answered. "Yeah, that's Sheri Summers. She works at the museum here in town. She really knows her stuff when it comes to history. If she says something's there, it probably is."

Jordan nodded and half smiled. "Is that right?" he muttered as he circled around to the side. She continued talking to the man leaning on the backhoe. Other workers who had gathered began to head back to the main work site. Jordan gazed down the length of her body. She certainly wasn't dressed for this confrontation. She wore a blue fitted skirt with a matching jacket, a white striped shirt and very high heels now covered in mud from the work site.

Her fervor seemed genuine. She appeared knowledgeable and determined to unearth whatever might be buried on the site. That intrigued him. Of course there was also her sexy body and air of self-confidence. He suddenly thought about what Ian had just said. Perhaps he wasn't experiencing enough of the local flavor.

"Look lady," the machine operator repeated, obviously having grown frustrated arguing with her. "It's just a bunch of old decayed wood tossed in a hole. You act like this is Noah's Ark or something."

"Noah's Ark isn't the only important ship in history. Have you ever heard of the *Amistad* or the *Zong?* They were also important ships. And both changed the course of history. At the time these ships reignited the abolitionist movement and are remembered for changing the course of history. And for your information this island was named after another very important slave ship. It was called the *Crescent.* But you wouldn't know anything about that, would you? That ship's history changed the lives of thousands of people and to this day is a little known piece of Civil War history. So as you can see, it's not just a bunch of wood, as you so callously put it. It might possibly be the most important piece of wood on this island."

Jordan knelt down and picked up a fragment of wood that had been pulled from the hole earlier that day. He examined it closely. It looked exactly like what it was, an old plank of waterlogged wood that had rotted and petrified over the decades. "What makes you think it's so important?" he asked, still feeling the rough edges of wood.

Sheri turned around quickly, seeing another construction worker kneeling down in the pile of debris. He was dressed like the others, jacket, jeans, work boots and hard hat. It looked as if he were trying to grow a beard and he had on dark sunglasses, so she couldn't see much of his face. But there was something very familiar about him.

"Well?" he prompted as he looked up at her.

"That's just it, Mr...." She paused.

"Hamilton. Jordan Hamilton," he said, standing up. "This is my development site."

Jordan Hamilton. Damn. Just like the last time, he took her breath away that fast. Good Lord. Yeah, she recognized him. He had a beard now, but even with the dark sunglasses and hard hat, she knew it was him. She remembered him, there was no way she'd forget, but apparently he didn't remember her since there was no sense of recognition in his face. She watched as his head dropped slightly. No one else noticed, but she did. He was checking her out just like he had before when Mamma Lou introduced them a few months ago. It was one of her matchmaking ploys, but it didn't work. Admittedly she was impressed when they met and apparently showed it. He went to get her a drink and returned with three women in tow. She just walked away.

"Mr. Hamilton, my name is Sheri Summers and this is my assistant, Genie Hopkins." She walked over, pulled out and handed him her business card. "We're here from the Crescent Island Museum because we think this may be an important find."

He took the card and looked it over. "It's not a find. It's a hole in the ground," he corrected, looking at the card the assistant had given him.

This she remembered well. He was arrogant and stubborn. "For you, maybe. But there is a very good possibility it's more than just a hole in the ground."

"But you don't know for sure," he responded.

And contrary. "No, not for sure, not yet. We'll

need to take samples, run tests and possibly excavate a portion of—"

"Excavate?"

And attractive. "Yes, but all that takes time. We're asking for that time. For something this important you must realize keeping this site intact is crucial. So, no we're not one hundred percent sure, but even the most remote possibility should be explored and not dismissed out of hand."

"So you do your tests and then what? In the meantime we're just supposed to stop working on your say-so?" he asked.

And sexy. She stiffened her chin firmly, more because of her own wayward thoughts than the discussion they were having. "I am highly qualified to make that call, if that's what you're implying."

He looked directly at her. "How?" he asked.

She frowned at him slightly confused by the question. "What do you mean, how?" she asked.

"I mean, how are you highly qualified?"

"I'm a historian, and an anthropologist and a museum curator. I run the historical department in the Crescent Island Museum. The museum is a branch of the Smithsonian for which I also work. I've studied all over the United States and around the world. However, my specific area of expertise is Virginia history with an emphasis on Crescent Island. I doubt anyone knows the history of this island better than I do."

"And your credentials…"

"Are impeccable, I assure you."

Jordan shook his head. "Sorry, that's not good enough," he said with a sense of authority. "It sounds like it's still just your word to me. Now if you'll excuse us, we have work to do." He stepped back and turned to leave.

Sheri took a deep breath then slowly released it. She was seething inside. Apparently he was going to make this impossible. It was obvious he had no intention of hearing her out. He'd already made up his mind. She glanced around. Most of the men who had been standing around had begun to move on. "With all due respect, Mr. Hamilton, it's not just my say-so," she called out, loud enough to stop him in his tracks. He turned back around. "It's the very real possibility of an extraordinary cultural discovery right here on this mound. However remote, it's still possible. I think that takes precedence over another concrete edifice to stroke some rich guy's superinflated ego."

A few of the men still standing around shook their heads and openly chuckled at the obvious slight meant for him. "Well," he said turning around to her, "be that as it may, that's just not good enough." He walked back over to her. The other men standing around instantly moved back, giving him space. "I see no reason to hold this up any longer. You had your say, now you need to step back and let my men do their jobs." He turned to the man now sitting in the backhoe. "Okay, Leroy, start it up, let's get this done." The machine roared to life again.

"No!" she yelled, stepping right into the path just as the machine lurched forward. "Wait!" She held her hands out as if to stop it all by herself. The shovel part of the backhoe jerked and slipped.

Jordan turned just as the shovel arm released. He dashed over and grabbed Sheri's waist and pulling her aside. "Are you insane or are you just off your meds this week? That machine could have killed you," he yelled over the loud noise the machine's engine made. "You can't just step in front of a moving piece of equipment like that. The shovel arm swings down automatically when the machine is turned on. Do you have any idea how dangerous that is? No, I don't suppose you do in your little history world." He was obviously furious.

Sheri's body shook as she realized what had just happened. "I wouldn't have to step in front of that backhoe if you would have just listened to me in the first place," she yelled back.

"I have listened to you. You made your point. Now it's your turn to listen to me. I'm not stopping this project for you or anyone else."

"You have no idea what you're about to do," she yelled.

"I'm about to get these men back to work," he replied.

"You're destroying history," she snapped.

"I'm building a resort," Jordan snapped back. The engine was still on and he impatiently waved to the man sitting in the cab of the machine. He shut the engine off.

"You're destroying history," she yelled again then lowered her voice as the engine subsided. By the time the machine's engine was completely silent, Jordan and Sheri were breathing hard as they glared at each other. Sheri looked down at his arm still around her. He was holding her close, too close, flush to his body. She looked back up at him. Her eyes were fiery. The corner of his lips twitched slightly. He released her slowly. Neither of them moved as they stared at each other face-to-face. He could swear he even heard her heart beating.

"Perhaps we should take this discussion into the office for a bit more privacy."

Sheri looked around at the small gathering that had been enjoying her tirade and the dramatic rescue. Some had even begun applauding. This wasn't what she intended. She was a professional, but his stubbornness made her so angry. She nodded curtly then followed him down the path to the trailer where she had waited earlier. "Sheri, I'll wait for you at the front gate, okay?" Genie said, standing with her boyfriend.

Sheri nodded as Jordan held the door for her. As soon as she passed him in the doorway she smelled the light woodsy scent of his cologne. It made her insides tingle, but she took a deep breath and calmed down. She started restating her case immediately. "First of all there's nothing arbitrary about my request. In my opinion…"

"You're different…" he said, smiling.

"What?"

"…than before when we met—you're different."

She smirked and shook her head. He did remember her. "No, I'm not different. I'm the same women you met and walked away from a few months ago."

"No, I'd remember that. You walked away from me."

"Then perhaps you didn't give yourself a chance to get to know me before forming an opinion about me."

"Perhaps I didn't. My bad."

"Getting back to our discussion…"

"And if in the end you find that it is just wood, what then?" he asked. "You would have cost this project hundreds of thousands of dollars in downtime and man-hours and delayed a project your board of supervisors agreed to back, then what?" She didn't respond. He nodded. "I didn't think so." He turned and walked over to his desk.

"I'm not on the board of supervisors, so I don't know what deals you made with them."

He whipped around and removed his sunglasses having felt the sting of her words hit too close to home. "I'm not in the habit of making deals with them or anyone else. I'm here to work and right now you're holding me up. So, unless you have a court order or a cease-and-desist letter, you're trespassing on private property. I'm gonna have to ask you to leave now." He walked back over to the door.

"You have no right to—"

"On the contrary, Ms. Summers, I have every right," he interrupted, clearly reaching his limit with the conversation.

"To destroy history," she challenged.

"To protect my property," he countered, "and right now this discussion is over."

"You can't do that," Sheri complained.

"You'd be surprised what I can do."

That, and the seductive crooked smile on his face, silenced her. Jordan walked over to his front door again. "But for decency's sake, I'll make sure to inform you when or if we pull anything out of the hole that looks like it's worth anything."

"Are you joking? No, absolutely not. That's not good enough. You're not a trained archaeologist. You have no idea what's of value and what's not. That's totally unacceptable."

"Right now that's all you've got. Take it or leave it."

She took a deep breath and glared at him. "I

guess I don't have much choice at the moment, do I?"

"There's always a choice."

"I want to be kept abreast of everything. If it comes out of that hole I want to know about it."

He nodded curtly then opened the trailer door, seeing Cleveland and Tamika standing outside talking. "Cleveland, please escort Ms. Summers and her associate to their car."

Sheri fumed as Cleveland stepped forward. She began walking then stopped as she passed Jordan in the doorway. She gazed up into his cold dark eyes. Her heart beat wildly and her stomach quivered. She was livid, but apparently he couldn't care less. "This isn't over," she assured him quietly.

He looked at her card and then smiled cockily as he saw the anger blaze in her eyes. He could plainly see she was furious, so he intentionally provoked her one last time. "I'd be greatly disappointed if it were."

She smiled tightly and then walked away.

Tamika walked toward Jordan. "Wow, what was all that?"

"A whole lot of interesting," he said admiringly.

Sheri was beyond furious by the time they reached the outside gate. He had challenged her and basically refused to budge. Her heart was thundering and it felt like every nerve in her body was on fire. She'd never been so infuriated in her life. And that was a major accomplishment considering who her former stepfather and her brothers were.

But his attitude was ten times worse. He was insulting and patronizing. And if he thought he'd won this war, he had another think coming. That was only the first battle and there was no way she was going to give up. When she said it wasn't over, she meant just that. "I can't believe the unmitigated gall of that man. He's a self-centered, closed-minded, egotistical jerk and he had the nerve to question my credentials. Who does he think he is?"

"Jordan Hamilton," Cleveland said. Both Sheri and Genie turned to look at him. He shrugged, having stated the obvious. "Ladies, have a good day," he said, as they exited the gate and continued to the Jeep.

Chapter 4

Jordan stood on the deck outside the trailer watching the fire-breathing Sheri storm away as he shook his head in exasperation. The whole situation would've been comical if it wasn't so ludicrous. Imagine, a woman coming out to his site to rage about a hole in the ground. He shook his head again. He'd certainly had his fill of drama for one day. He walked out onto the deck then went down the steps to watch her walk away. Cleveland led the two women down the muddy path. When they reached the asphalt she turned around. They stared at each other a moment across the short distance. Neither gestured or said anything, but each knew exactly what the other was thinking. She had thrown down the proverbial gauntlet and he had eagerly picked it up. He smiled knowingly, realizing he meant exactly what he said—he would be disappointed if this was over.

He liked her fire. And he liked the passion he saw in her eyes. Just watching her now sent a slow burn down the center of his body. Maybe Ian was right, maybe he had been out of circulation too long. Either way she was working his body like a full-time job and then some. His mouth dried and he licked his lips. Her reaction was instant.

He chuckled to himself. There was something about the fire in her eyes that intrigued him. He liked it. He also liked the way his body had burned when he held her. She was certainly brazen to come out here like that. Most women he'd known would have never jeopardized a pair of heels for any cause. They'd back away from confrontation, but she stood right up to him. No woman had ever spoken to him like that. They usually did whatever he wanted, no matter what it was. But somehow he knew she'd be different and he liked the challenge before they even began.

Cleveland stepped up, said something to her and then led them back onto the walkway then around the office trailers toward the front gate. When they rounded the corner and disappeared from sight, Jordan shook his head again. Long shapely legs planted in high stiletto heels covered in red clay and sand. It had to take some kind of dedication to make a woman stand in the middle of a construction site dressed like that.

He knew the type, a woman on a mission, fanatical, obsessive and self-righteous in her beliefs for a cause. She reminded him of someone he once knew. And apparently Sheri Summers's cause had something to do with a hole in the ground. He'd give her three days. By the weekend she would have certainly given up. But he momentarily reconsidered. That kind of passion wasn't easily discouraged. He knew she'd be back.

He walked back up to the secondary site and looked down into the hole. The machine across from him roared to life again and took his attention away from his wandering thoughts. He waved for the man in the backhoe to cut the engine again. He walked over to the pile of wooden planks then turned to the machine operator. "Did anything else come out of that hole?" he asked.

"Nah, it's just a bunch of old wood and some trash," he said. "Empty soda bottles, cans, vines, tumbled limbs and a ton of crushed-up wood, you know, the usual stuff," he called down. "I don't get why all the drama over what was probably an old forgotten trash dump?"

Jordan shook his head. It didn't make any sense. "Do me a favor, Leroy. Drain the rest of the hole.

I want to see what's really down there. And make sure everything pulled out of there goes to the office, no matter how insignificant it appears."

Leroy looked at the pile of trash. "I found a glass bottle floating in there. It was old, like one of those old-fashioned medicine bottles. I pulled it out and tossed it on the side. It's gone now. One of the workers might have grabbed it."

"Who?" Jordan said, immediately finding that unacceptable.

"One of the new guys," Leroy said. "He mentioned he wanted a glass bottle to give to his girlfriend."

"Find out who it was and make sure whatever was found is in the trailer by the end of the week."

Leroy nodded, hopped down and headed to the pump generator to begin draining the remainder of the water. Jordan watched the draining for a few moments. "What's that?"

Leroy squinted. "I don't know. Looks like bucket."

Jordan leaned down to pull it out, but it didn't budge. "Hold on, let me use the backhoe," Leroy said. He climbed up, turned the machine on and easily dug out the bucket and surrounding dirt. He unloaded it beside the other debris.

As soon as Leroy dropped the shovel there was a loud crack and the machine stalled and began smoking.

"Hold it, hold it. Cut it off." The engine sputtered then slowly died. "What was that?"

"I don't know. It did that earlier, too. Whatever it is down there just cracked the arm again. I used the last replacement part. It'll probably take a few days to get another one here and all the larger machines are already off-site."

Jordan walked over, picked it up, cleaned it off and looked at it. It wasn't a bucket. It was a bell. He turned it over several times and tried unsuccessfully to scrape away some of the caked-on mud. "Okay, get Tamika to order the part. And better get a spare. We'll hold up digging around this area until the replacement part is in."

Leroy nodded. "All right."

Jordan turned and headed back to the trailer. As soon he sat down at his desk the phone rang. He pulled it out and, seeing the caller ID, answered. "Hi, bro, what's up?"

"Wow, you answered, I'm surprised. I've been calling you all day. I assumed your phone was sitting at the bottom of a cement mixer," his brother said in his usual sarcastic manner.

Jordan chuckled. "Yeah, yeah, I know. I meant to call you back earlier. So what's up?" Jordan asked.

"Nothing much, how's everything there?" Darius said.

Jordan looked around the office thinking about Sheri. A slow easy smile tipped his full lips. He picked up and toyed with the business card her assistant had given him. "Not bad at all."

"Good, listen, what are your plans this evening?"

"I'm just headed home, why?"

"Good, I need a favor."

"Sure, what kind of favor?" Jordan asked as he typed in a web address, pressed the enter key and waited a second as the Crescent Island Museum website came up.

"I need you to pick something up for me. It's on the way."

"Okay, what and where?" Jordan said.

"It's right there on Crescent Island."

"Here?"

"Yes, it's at Gates Manor, Louise Gates's home. She called me earlier this afternoon. She has some paperwork for me."

Jordan stopped pressing keys and just sat there. "You're kidding, right? Louise Gates has something for you."

Darius started chuckling.

"You know what she's like. She's a self-professed matchmaker," Jordan said. "She was practically taking notes at Dillon's fourth birthday party last year."

"Actually, she *was* taking notes," Darius corrected him, still chuckling.

"This isn't funny," Jordan declared. "I thought Aunt Ellen was bad, she's nothing compared to

Mamma Lou. The people on this island adore her. You should hear them. They think she's magical with her matchmaking." Darius continued laughing. "And it's not funny."

"Come on, man, since when are you afraid of an eighty-year-old woman? You can handle her."

"That's not the point. Why put myself on her radar?"

"Truthfully, bro, you and I already are."

"Yeah, I know. So why tempt fate? I gotta steer clear."

"Can't do that," Darius said. "I need that paperwork tonight."

"She can email or fax it to you."

"I need the originals."

"Fine, she can send it overnight express. They'll get to the office first thing in the morning. Better yet, I'll pay for a door-to-door courier."

"Nope, I need them tonight."

Jordan sighed deeply. "Come on man, you're killing me."

"I wouldn't ask if they weren't important."

"All right, I'll do it. But you owe me big-time for this one."

"I know. I'll see you later."

Jordan closed his cell phone and sat back in his chair. He shook his head. The thought of being anywhere near Louise Gates made him nervous. He had no idea how his brother Julian did it. But now he supposed Julian had nothing to fear, being married to Dena. It wasn't until after the wedding that they found out Louise Gates had played matchmaker all along. But to her credit she'd certainly gotten it right. He'd never seen his brother so happy. Still he had no intention of being her next target. Fine, he'd go and pick up the paperwork for his brother. But as far as getting caught up in Mamma Lou's matchmaking schemes, he would definitely steer clear.

Chapter 5

Genie didn't start the engine right away. They just sat there in the car, staring out the front windshield mostly in shock. "Wow, that was really intense," she said breathlessly.

"Yeah, it was too intense," Sheri replied. Her heart was still beating like crazy. "I can't believe I got so angry and he actually had security escort us out."

"What a rush," Genie added excitedly, putting her key in the ignition without turning it. "I thought stuff like that only happened in the movies. Being an archaeologist really is exciting."

Sheri took a deep breath and released it slowly.

"Okay, this obviously didn't go as expected. Still, nothing's really changed," she said confidently. "I'm going to do exactly what we intended to do. I'm going to stop them from destroying that site. Granted, it isn't going to be easy and it certainly doesn't look like Jordan Hamilton is going to listen to reason."

"Yeah, you got that right," Genie said. "But bottom line, he was right, it's private property and he can do whatever he wants on his property. We can't actually force him to comply."

"I'll call the Smithsonian and let them know what's going on," Sheri said. "Their lawyers should be able to do something about this, but it's going to take time."

"But what if we don't have time?" Genie said impatiently.

"The museum will be fine. Don't worry," Sheri said, as the wheels turned in her head.

"I don't know about that. I've heard that situations like this get bogged down in bureaucratic red tape and then nothing gets done. Money changes hands and eventually everything just gets swept under the rug and buried. What we need is to act fast, right now, immediately," she said excitedly.

"Genie, calm down. There's a way to handle this. We have to follow the proper procedures."

"Okay, okay, I get it. So short of kidnapping Hamilton and holding him ransom to get what we want, what do we do in the meantime? Please don't tell me we just get to sit around and do nothing?"

"No, we do our work and we follow the rules and gather as much information on the *Crescent* ship as we can. If the Smithsonian lawyers are going to do battle with Jordan Hamilton and his high-priced attorneys, we need our side to be as prepared as possible. Nobody knows this island's history better than I do."

"Okay, that sounds good." Genie put the Jeep in gear and pulled out of the parking lot. They drove in silence for a while, each reflecting on what had just happened at the site. Genie started talking about everything that happened. She was getting more and more excited.

Sheri gazed out the window, seeing the sights of Crescent Island pass by. It was peaceful and tranquil outside, but there was still an unsettling feeling. Gone was her usual excitement and energy. The island seemed to have slowed to a sigh as the last signs of summer clung to the trees and the quiet of fall's approach hovered all around. This was her favorite time of year. The weather wasn't cold yet, but there was a bit of a nip in the air. That's exactly how she liked it. It was as if the whole island was preparing for the next season.

"Man, this would have been so cool if it happened next month instead of today. Then we could have let Mother Nature take its course. Let's see the great and powerful Jordan Hamilton dig through snow, ice and frozen ground," Genie joked.

The thought made Sheri smile. "Fortunately for him the weather's usually not that bad here. It gets cold and we sometimes have snow, but not a lot and not often. Even when Washington gets hit hard, we barely get a dusting. That's probably why they chose this site."

"You know it's a shame he had to be so mean about this. He could have been a terrific patron to the museum."

"What?" Sheri said, paying attention again.

"He has money and power."

"I guess," Sheri said.

"No, really. He's professional, intelligent and he looks like he can get things done. Besides that, the brother is fine."

"What do his looks have to do with anything?"

"Nothing, I just like looking at him," Genie said, and giggled.

"I'll chalk that up to youth."

"Oh, come on. You know he's gorgeous."

"He's all right," Sheri said nonchalantly.

"I saw his picture in the newspaper a couple of times, so I kinda knew who he was when he stood up and started talking. But I seriously didn't think he was going to be that gorgeous in person. He's like a walking wet dream. Dark, sultry bedroom eyes and a strong, muscular build. He's the perfect male specimen. And I really liked that rugged, half-shaven look on him. What do you think?"

"I wasn't paying much attention," Sheri said dismissively.

Genie looked over at her. "Oh, please, who are you trying to fool? Tall, dark, handsome, a great physique and he's rich. That's like the Mega Millions of single guys these days. How in the world were you not paying attention? When a man looks like that, everybody pays attention. And you were right up in the man's face."

"Yes, and if you remember correctly we weren't exactly chatting. We were right in the middle of a heated argument."

"Heated is the operative word. And if the look in his eyes was any indication, you two had some serious heat going on. As a matter of fact, when that backhoe was turned on and you were right up there in his face, I would have sworn you two were about to do something other than argue."

"What do you mean, do something other than argue?"

"Do I have to spell it out?" Genie asked rhetorically. Sheri's expression didn't change. "Fine, it looked like you two were about to jump each other's bones and get busy right there."

"What? Oh, no, you did not just say that," Sheri countered. "Uh-uh, no way."

"I don't know. Passion works in strange ways.

And you two had some serious heat going on up there."

"Passion is not that strange, and the heat was certainly not mine," Sheri assured her.

"Still, I guess if all else fails you'll at least get close to him."

"And then what?"

"Duh, Sheri, has it been that long? Use your feminine wiles. Seduce the man. Do a little give-and-take."

Sheri laughed out loud. "No, I don't think so," she said.

"Why not?" Genie asked.

"Because it would be demeaning and degrading, and besides, trust me, I am most definitely not that man's type."

"How do you know you're not his type?" Genie asked as she parked the Jeep in her spot behind the museum. They got out and walked around to the front of the building.

"It's obvious. He's got an ego the size of North America."

"Actually that might bode well for other parts of his anatomy," Genie joked.

"Would you stop with the sex talk, please? Anyway, as you say, he's a rich, single and used to getting what he wants. That means his type of woman is everything I'm not—specifically, an airhead. His ideal woman probably caters to him twenty-four hours a day. I'm not the submissive type. I have a brain and know how to use it."

"He could surprise you."

"Trust me, he wouldn't have a clue as to what to do with a woman like me," she said, walking up the steps to the front entrance.

Genie followed close. "He's a man, I think he would. The question is would you know what to do with a man like him?"

Sheri turned, opened her mouth then quickly closed it and stumbled, catching herself before she fell. "Okay, why are we even speculating about this? It's a nonissue. It's not gonna happen. Trust me. The only thing I want from Jordan Hamilton is sitting in the bottom of a hole on his property."

They walked through the employee area of the museum as they headed toward the stairs. "So, what are you going to do now?" Genie asked.

"First, I'll call Jack McDonald at the Smithsonian and let him know what's going on. There's nothing we can really do until I speak with him. I have a few more things to take care of here at the office. The running of this museum still goes on. My main concerns are the revised budget report and the funding we need to secure. I have to get next year's budget together as soon as possible," she said as they went into her office.

"Yeah, but what about the site? What do we do about it?"

"Nothing right now," she said.

Genie's eyes widened in shock. "Nothing? But there are valuable artifacts there."

"That's why we have to tread lightly and do everything by the book."

Genie folded her arms over her chest. It was obvious she wasn't buying the wait-and-see answer. "I don't get it. Why even have a museum if people are just going to bulldoze over everything anyway? It's like we don't have a say on our own island. How can this even happen?"

Sheri shook her head. "Unfortunately this happens a lot. Development companies purchase land and begin construction only to find a cemetery or a piece of history long forgotten buried on that land. Regrettably, it's usually covered up and all the artifacts and finds are discarded without the proper authorities ever knowing about it."

"But we do know and we need to move quickly."

"It isn't that easy, Genie."

"I don't see why not," she insisted.

Sheri smiled. She remembered Genie's exuberance and impatience well. She was about the same age as her assistant when the *Mabella Louisa* was discovered off the coast of Crescent Island and the small, almost insignificant museum was added to the Smithsonian Institution because of the find. Maybe, just maybe it would stay whatever change she knew was coming.

Sheri sat down, put her elbows on the desk and covered her face. A lot of what Genie said was right. She also felt the same outrage and anger Genie did. But she couldn't lose sight of what was important. Right now Jordan Hamilton held all the cards. She needed to be calm and get this worked out. She also knew she had to do something now.

Sheri grabbed the cell phone and made her first call, Jack McDonald at the Smithsonian. Although Jack was not a curator or historian, his position as registrar meant he was the supervisor for a number of smaller off-site museums. His voice mail picked up and she left a message. "Jack, hi. It's Sheri. Please give me a call back as soon as you can. It's very important. Thank you."

As soon as she hung up there was a knock at her door. She smiled when she saw her grandmother's best friend standing in the doorway. "Mamma Lou, hi."

"Hello, dear, I hope I'm not disturbing you," Louise said.

"No, not at all. Come in, have a seat," she said, standing and walking around to the front of her desk. She gave the spry octogenarian a hug and pulled a chair out for her. Sheri looked back to the office door as Louise sat down. "Where's Colonel Wheeler?"

"He'll be here in a few minutes. He's downstairs talking with an old friend. I declare, no matter where we go Otis always runs into someone he knows. It's absolutely amazing. It never fails. But actually today it's a good thing, I told him to take his time, so we can have a few minutes for girl talk."

After Louise sat down Sheri went back to her desk. "It's good to see you, Mamma Lou."

"You, too. Camille and I were chatting this morning and since I told her I'd be in town today she suggested I stop by and peek in on you this afternoon."

Sheri shook her head. Her grandmother always knew when she needed something. "I'm glad you did. It's good to see you, Mamma Lou. I think I can use a friendly face right about now." Her voice trailed off softly. Louise noticed instantly.

"It looks like Camille was right. You look troubled."

"I am. I just got back from Crescent Point and meeting with Jordan Hamilton," Sheri began. Louise smiled. "No, Mamma Lou, it's not what you think, trust me. I know you hoped at one time that he and I were a match, but believe me we're not. You're completely off on this one. We couldn't be further apart. He's the absolute last man on earth for me."

"Are you sure about that?" Louise asked as she remembered seeing the sparks of attraction in their eyes as soon as she introduced them at the party she gave months ago. It was unmistakable. She knew instinctively they were the perfect match. Unfortunately sometimes people fought so hard to stay apart that they nearly missed what was right in front of them. She had no intention of letting that happen to Sheri and Jordan.

"I'm completely sure. The man's impossible. Talking to him is like banging your head against a brick wall. He's stubborn and arrogant, and as far as I'm concerned he has no values, no ethics. I don't know how anybody can actually work for him. He must be a tyrant."

"That doesn't sound like the Jordan Hamilton I know."

"Trust me, it is."

"Has something happened that I don't know about?"

Sheri spent the next ten minutes telling Louise exactly what happened at the construction site earlier. Louise asked a few questions and Sheri answered, trying her best to sound as unbiased as possible.

"My goodness," Louise said. "The possibility of discovering the *Crescent* would be absolutely extraordinary. A find of this enormity couldn't go unrecognized. It's our collective responsibility to do something, at least to make sure one way or the other."

"I agree. But right now I'm at a loss. Jordan Hamilton is impossible."

"That's so unlike him. He and his brothers are wonderful, very caring and charitable men."

"Not in this case, not him. I have a phone call in to Jack in D.C. and I'm going to speak with Nolan later today and see what he can do to help. I'm also going to speak with Uncle Hal. My last resort is to get an injunction or something like that."

"An injunction is pretty severe, don't you think?"

"No, not at all. Jordan Hamilton was very emphatic about his position. He's not going to allow us back on his property."

"I see. Well, speaking with your uncle is certainly an idea. I'm sure he'll be able to mediate a resolution. But before you turn to such drastic measures, perhaps you'd allow me to possibly mediate a solution. Have you spoken to Jordan since this happened?"

"No, not really," she said.

"Sometimes a nice quiet conversation is all that's needed in situations like this. I'll call and speak with him."

"I doubt you'll get very far, Mamma Lou. Jordan Hamilton is the most, annoying, stubborn, insolent man I've ever met. He's a total jerk."

"Is that so?" Louise said with added interest, trying her best not to appear as pleased as she was. To some without an ear for what was really going on, the conversation sounded hopeless. But she knew better. Her plan was working out even better than she'd hoped.

"Well, aside from all that, I'll call and see what I can do. I'd like to also suggest that you contact him," she added. Sheri began shaking her head. "Just one phone call, Sheri. It's asking so little to gain so much."

Sheri finally nodded in agreement. "Okay, I'll do it. Thank you, Mamma Lou. Still, I wouldn't get your hopes up. But of course I appreciate whatever you can do."

"Well, I'd better get out of here and get busy. We both have a lot of work to do. And if we could have some kind of solution by the sesquicentennial celebration, that would be wonderful." She stood. Sheri walked her to the door. "Please keep me posted on your progress."

"I will. Thanks again, Mamma Lou. I'll talk to you soon."

Louise turned in the doorway. "Remember, we aren't always who we seem to others. Look below the surface and see the man I know is there. Call him. Talk to him. You'll work this out."

Sheri nodded but knew there was no way she and Jordan Hamilton would ever be able to come to an understanding.

Jordan finally caught up with his brother Julian. He needed to vent and Julian was the perfect person to listen. He picked up on the first ring. "Hey, what's up?" Julian said.

"It's been one of those days. How are Dena and Dillon?"

"Fine, Dillon's getting bigger and bigger every minute. I swear he's amazing. He begs to go to work with me every day and his eyes light up as soon as we pull into the lot. You know he wants his own desk at the office."

Jordan laughed. It was the best thing he'd heard all day. "Yeah, now that's what I'm talking 'bout. Sounds like we already have the next generation of Hamilton Development ready to go."

"Yeah, well, I'm doing my part."

"All right, don't get all Mamma Lou on me."

It was Julian's turn to laugh. "Well, it took her long enough."

"What do you mean?" Jordan asked.

"You know she's had her sights on you and Darius ever since she found out I had two single brothers."

"Nah, I've been blocking her for the past five months."

"She's good, man. Trust me. If it wasn't for Mamma Lou I would have never met Dena. She changed my life and I realized that everything I thought I wanted wasn't what I needed. I've never been happier."

"And I'm happy for you, man, but that's not me. I'm not the family kind of guy, you know that."

"Yeah, but I remember saying the exact same thing. So, how's everything going there?" Julian asked.

"The deadline is going to be tight, but we'll meet it."

"Excellent."

"Now if I can just get rid of the distractions," he added.

"What kind of distractions?" Julian asked. "Now you know that's never going to happen."

"I can dream. It seems every other day I get a phone call from a member of the board of supervisors. Today I spent all morning and most of the afternoon listening to a couple of whiny politicians trying to alter my plans and then asking for handouts. Seriously, to hear them talk, you'd think it was their project."

Julian laughed. "Come on, it couldn't have been that bad."

"Trust me, it was worse. You know the drill, supervisors, board of directors, city hall politicians. They all want something for nothing. Today it was concessions and payoffs in exchange for smoothing the way with utilities, regulators and inspectors."

"Yep, that sounds about right," Julian said, chuckling. "So, what did these guys want?"

"You name it, they wanted it. Personal suites in

the resort, lifetime spa memberships, preferential treatment on-site, the works. Oh, wait, and my personal favorite, I've been asked if a few of my workers could stop by one of their homes and renovate their kitchen."

Julian laughed again. "Free of charge, I assume."

"Oh, you know that," Jordan said, joining his brother's laughter.

"You know it's pretty much expected. We get these requests all the time. There are always one or two politicians in every city we've done business who want to make a side deal or get some kind of kickback. It's the nature of the business. I hope you were polite when you turned them down."

"Actually, no, I wasn't in the mood to play nice."

"Okay, what exactly did you do?" he asked.

"I told them what I thought. Perhaps I was a bit abrupt."

"What does 'a bit abrupt' mean?"

"I excused myself and walked out to take care of an urgent situation on-site. It's an old dodge, but it always works."

"You know you have to do something about that. We need these people to get the job finished. You've played the game long enough to know that."

"Yeah, yeah, I know. I'll take care of it later," he said drily. "That reminds me, a woman came by the site this afternoon..." Jordan began.

Julian started chuckling immediately. He knew

his brother too well. When it came to women he was the ultimate player.

"Believe me, it's not one of those stories. To tell you the truth, I'm really not sure what to make of her. My gut feeling tells me she's trouble."

"What do you mean?"

"Her name is Sheri Summers. She's from the local museum and she seems to think there might be some historical artifacts in a hole on the secondary site."

"How does she know that?"

"That's what I was wondering. Apparently someone on-site told her."

"So you dug them up?" Julian asked.

"No, we cleared debris and overgrown foliage last week then it rained a few days and eroded one of the holes at the secondary site. I had it drained and it looks like planks of wood began showing up, along with an old medicine bottle."

"It doesn't sound like much."

"I agree. It could be anything. But just in case, I'm gonna put a call into Kenneth and stop by an antique shop in town. The last thing we need is more legal delays."

"Good idea."

"So, how's it going in D.C.? Any word yet?"

"No word yet. But it's looking really good. We made it through to the final two cut. I think we have a really good shot at getting this bid. It's a major contract and along with the Crescent Island project, it could very well set us up nicely for the future. The bid and proposal were right on target and the architectural renderings you did were exactly what they were looking for. I think we just might have this one."

"Excellent," Jordan said happily. He needed to hear some good news after the day he had. It wasn't that the company was doing badly or anything. But having the next project set up and waiting was always good business. With the economy still sluggish and the housing and commercial construction markets stalled, getting new projects was becoming more and more difficult.

He knew what the market had done to a lot of companies their size. Some were bankrupt and others were working on a shoestring with less than half their staff. Hamilton Development had been blessed. Their business had increased and they'd been steadily working and even hiring more workers. "That's really great news."

"All right, I gotta go. Duty calls."

"All right, man. Thanks, talk to you later."

Jordan hung up feeling a lot better. He was ready to take on the world again. That included Nolan, the board of supervisors and, especially, Sheri Summers.

Chapter 6

Jordan went back to work after his brother's phone call. After a few hours of work he got up, grabbed a bottle of water from the office refrigerator and carried it to his desk. He sat down, opened it and took a long sip while thinking about his earlier altercation with Sheri Summers. He smiled. She was a lot different than he remembered. He reached over and turned on his computer as he began dialing the phone. A few seconds later Kenneth Fields answered. "Kenneth, it's Jordan."

"Hey buddy, what's up? How are you? Where are you now?"

"I'm doing okay. I'm at the Crescent Island property."

"How's the project coming?"

"Good. We've made amazing progress since you were last here. We should be finishing up soon."

"Any more problems with the locals?" he asked.

"No, nothing too major, nothing we can't handle on-site."

"Good, so what can I do for you?" Kenneth asked.

"I'm not sure if this is anything or not, but I wanted to keep you in the loop and I wanted your thoughts."

"Sure, what's happening?" Kenneth asked.

"I just had a visit from a woman who works at the local museum. She was very upset and she seems to think that there may be some artifacts of historical significance at our secondary site. We're just about to get started in that area in couple of weeks, and with our tight schedule I can't afford any delays."

"What makes her think there are artifacts on the site?"

"Some bush was cleared and a hole was dug earlier. We had a few days of hard rain and we came across some wooden planks and what looks like an old medicine bottle and a ship's bell."

"Not exactly a smoking gun, but curious nonetheless. When the land was purchased a thorough title search was performed. Due diligence came up blank. We can only depend on the available records from local officials. The previous building and land maps showed no unusual certifications. At this point I wouldn't worry too much about it. It's not a legal issue. I will however make some inquiries on this end. I have a few friends in the Library for Research in African Culture. But do me a favor, keep track of everything you find and pull out of there. Write down specifics, time, date, location, who found them, et cetera."

"Will do. Anything else?"

"Yeah, keep a close eye on the site for a while, maybe beef up security the next few days. If people think there's something of value out there, you might run into some trouble with the locals and those looking to cash in. Treasure hunting is always a draw for some."

"Yeah, I already have security on it."

"Good. Let me know if you have any other problems."

"I will. Thanks."

"What time are you getting in this evening?"

"Not until late. I have a few things to take care of before I leave, and Darius asked me to pick up some documents from Louise Gates."

Kenneth started laughing. "That's pretty brave of you."

"Yeah, tell me about it. The woman has matchmaking on the mind twenty-four-seven."

"Didn't she already try to set you up a while ago?"

Jordan chuckled. "Yeah, but it didn't work out. We weren't exactly compatible at the time. Coincidently, she's the woman I told you about from the museum."

"Interesting coincidence. Are you sure this isn't one of Louise Gates's matchmaking schemes?"

"Nah, not this time. She doesn't know anything about what's going on here at the site. And besides, Sheri Summer was just as adamant about staying single as I am. That's about the only thing we can actually agree upon."

"Still…"

"Yeah, I know," Jordan agreed. "I'm watching my back. I'll talk to you when I get there this evening." Jordan closed his cell and took another sip of water. He saw the business card he had tossed on his desk earlier. He picked it up and read the raised lettering. He started typing in the web address but then stopped when his cell phone rang. He expected more drama. "Yeah," he said gruffly.

"You got a minute? I'm on the main floor," Ian said.

"On my way," Jordan said. He grabbed the floor plans and went to the primary site. He ran into Ian and Cleveland talking on the main floor. The first thing he noticed was the faint smell of smoke.

"Everything okay in here?" Jordan asked, grimacing.

"Yeah, no problems now. We have a new generator and some oil spilled on the coils. It started smoking. Everything's under control now, but this shouldn't have happened. The coils were clean when the unit was installed two weeks ago."

"Are we having problems again?" Jordan asked.

"I'm not sure," Ian said.

"I'll up security and increase the foot patrol just in case," Cleveland said. "If there's a problem, my guys will find it and take care of it."

Jordan nodded and took a deep breath. "I guess it's going to be one of those days."

"Oh, yeah, looks like it," Ian added.

Jordan looked around with his usual critical eye. When it came to his work, everything had to be perfect. But now that this was a Hamilton Development Corporation–owned project he had to step up his game and take it beyond just perfection. The future of the company—everything—was riding on this. Hamilton Resort Complex had to be magnificent.

Everything seemed to be close to schedule. The drywall was up, the windows and doors were in, electrical, plumbing and HVAC systems were all installed and operational. The flooring specialists were preparing to put in stone and hardwoods. He was pleased with what he saw. "It's definitely looking good in here. Minus any more drama, we just might pull this off."

Ian nodded. "I agree. This is by far the most ambitious project to date and we're knocking it out of the ballpark. It's going to be awesome." They discussed a few technical details then headed back outside. "So, I heard you made yourself a new friend today. Not bad," Ian said, smiling broadly, obviously trying hard not to laugh.

"You heard that, huh?"

"Oh, yeah, I think everybody in the company did," Ian said, giving in to his suppressed chuckle.

"Everybody?" Jordan questioned, turning to him.

"Well, maybe not everybody. There are a couple of workers off today. But I think someone sent them a cell phone video."

"There's a video?" Jordan asked, surprised. He stopped walking then saw Ian laughing. "Damn, that's the last thing I need."

"Man, you know with the internet and YouTube, everything we do goes public. So what was all the drama about?"

Jordan shook his head. "I don't know. Some woman, Sheri Summers, she works at the local museum and for some reason she seems to think there's something in that hole worth preserving."

"Is there?"

"I don't know and the last thing I need right now

are last-minute surprises. I guess I'm gonna have to look into it, or…"

"Or what?" Ian asked then quickly answered. "No, don't tell me, let me guess. Or you'll just pour on the charm like you always do and have her eating out of your hand in no time."

"I wouldn't put it that directly, but, yeah, something along those lines. I can handle women. That's what I do."

Ian shook his head. "One of these days you're going to run into a woman you can't manipulate and charm. And she's going to capture your heart before you even know it. You're gonna be head over heels in love."

Jordan laughed heartily. He knew there was no way he'd allow that to happen. He would never allow himself to fall in love. There had been other women in his life who had tried. They all tried and they all failed. There was no way it was going to happen. He guarded his heart too closely and no woman was ever going to get to him.

"Okay, you laugh now, but mark my words, one of these days it'll happen. Love will happen."

"Trust me. That will never happen. You know I don't do the love thing. I leave that to Julian and Darius. Not me, never me."

Ian shook his head. "You know better than that, never say never."

"Never," Jordan said defiantly.

"Now you're just tempting fate. But all right, you got that. In the meantime, I need to check on some supplies I ordered for the rest of the week. I'll be off-site the rest of the day. You headed back to the main office?"

"Nah, I'm gonna hang around here for the next few hours."

"All right, I'll catch up with you tomorrow."

"All right, I'll see you later," Jordan said as his cell rang. He pulled it out and answered. "Jordan Hamilton."

"Jordan, this is Nolan Chambers. I'm glad I caught you before you left for the day. I was wondering if you could stop by my office this evening. I think we need to talk."

He didn't have to ask what this was about—he knew. But he wasn't in the mood to deal with Nolan at the moment. "I have another appointment this evening, Nolan."

"I understand, but this is important. I believe our discussion this morning ended awkwardly to say the least. Neither one of us should be taking a hit for this. Now I'm going to help you all I can, but you need to meet me halfway. I'm sure a few very minor concessions aren't completely out of the question. After all we both want the same thing, for Hamilton Resort Complex to be a success. The board would like you to know that we have the utmost respect for you and your company. We'd like nothing better than to have this Hamilton Development project completed with few to no unscheduled delays. And of course we'd love to have more projects here on Crescent Island."

The veiled threat wasn't so veiled. "What do you propose?"

"If you could stop by my office we could talk privately. I'd like to explain our position in more detail."

"Fine, I'll meet you tomorrow."

"Uh, perhaps we can make it sooner, possibly this evening," Nolan suggested.

Jordan stalled on purpose then finally agreed to meet him.

"Excellent, that will be fine. I had a meeting in Richmond today and I'm headed back to the island now. Can we make it let's say, six-thirty?"

"Yeah, okay."

"Excellent, I'll meet you around six-thirty this evening."

"Fine," Jordan confirmed then hung up. He went back to the trailer office, sat down and opened his laptop. He took a deep breath and dived back in.

As an architect, his job was basically done. But as general contractor, he was responsible for building and seeing the project through to completion. He worked the rest of the day thankfully in nearly uninterrupted peace. He followed up on requests and orders, reviewed the budget, status and technical reports and completed a number of tasks he had put off all last week. It was time to get back to work.

Sheri stared at the computer monitor for the next hour and a half. There were figures she had to identify and a report she needed to write, but it was no use. All she kept thinking about was seeing Jordan again. Her heart was still beating fast.

Genie was right. He was gorgeous. But he was also impossible. His absolute refusal to listen to her request was infuriating. It was like he intentionally dismissed her. She shook her head to try and refocus on the job at hand. She read the screen then revised a few paragraphs. A few seconds later she deleted what she'd written and revised it again. Just as she finished her thought her phone rang. She glanced at the caller ID then picked up quickly. "Sheri Summers."

"Sheri, hi, it's Jack."

"Hi, Jack, thanks for getting back to me."

"No problem. Look, I know what you're gonna ask me. I received all three of your requisitions. But I'm sorry I can't give you any more money than I already have. The building is falling down around you and it's only getting worse. The budget is extremely tight this year and we're struggling to make ends meet over here. Unfortunately, donations aren't what they used to be."

"No, Jack, that's not what I need to talk to you about. I need you to contact legal with a formal request. We might have a situation here."

"What's the problem?" he asked. She spent the next five minutes telling him in detail about the photos and what had happened at the work site. "What's the name of this construction company?"

"It's called Hamilton Development."

There was a brief pause. "Wait, do you mean Hamilton Development out of Northern Virginia?"

"Yes, I think so. Do you know of them?"

"Yes, of course I do. They're very good friends of the museum here in D.C. They are very generous in giving to the museum's program sponsorship."

"I'm guessing that changes things," she said, already disappointed and knowing exactly where this conversation was going.

"No, not necessarily," Jack said. "I'm sure we can work all this out amicably without contacting legal."

"I already tried," she said. "He won't listen to me."

"Perhaps I should speak to Darius. He's my main contact."

"But he's not the brother doing the work, it's Jordan."

"Oh, then, I'm sure there must be some mistake. I've met Jordan. He's extremely generous with his time and talent both personally and professionally."

"Jack, it's not about giving money right now, it's about finding the historical remains of a ship on his property, a very important ship, one that defined this island."

"Yes, yes, I understand that. But perhaps we can find a better solution than bringing this up to legal. I suggest we take our time with this."

Sheri rolled her eyes to the ceiling. She expected Jack to drag his feet. She just didn't expect him to completely wimp out on her. "We may not have time, Jack. They could bulldoze the area and cover that hole up any day now, if it hasn't already been done. We would have lost a major historical find in the process."

"I'm sure that won't happen. Jordan is very sensitive to the museum," he insisted. "I don't know if you remember this but we had a situation like this a few years back and—"

"Yeah, I remember," she interrupted quickly. "It was in Haymarket near the battlefield. A developer wanted to build homes and they found artifacts on the property."

"Exactly, and it turned into a public relations nightmare. We lost millions of dollars in funding. If we make the wrong move here, this will blow up in our faces."

"But we have to do something."

"We will, we will. I'm just not all that sure what it might be at this point. Let me confer with a few people here and see what we can come up with. Just hold on, do nothing for right now."

"How long will it take?"

"I don't know, a week, perhaps two or more."

"Jack…" she began.

"Sheri, don't worry, I got this. I'll take care of it."

That's when she started worrying. She knew there was going to be a delay. She'd run into situations like this with him before. He was useless when it came to actually doing something to help. When Jack didn't want to deal with something, he would just let the situation fester, ignore it as if it hadn't happened and hope for the best. It was a ridiculous way to manage museums, but when your mother sits on the board of directors and you have no professional qualifications for the post, ignoring it was the best he could do. "All right, thanks, Jack. Please keep me in the loop on this."

"Sure, sure, we'll talk later."

Sheri hung up and sighed heavily. It looked like Genie was right. With Jack at the helm, this was going to turn into a bureaucratic nightmare. He had no idea what it meant to love art and history and what it meant to want to preserve the past. All he cared about was impressing the higher-ups, coming in under budget and making as few waves as possible in the process.

It was obvious she needed some kind of backup

plan. But right now she had no idea what she was going to do or how she was going to do it. She looked up at the computer monitor. It had gone to sleep. She pressed a key on her keyboard and went back to work knowing she'd come up with something, even if it took her the rest of the afternoon. Much to her dismay, it did and she still had no plan.

As usual Sheri stayed late. She worked on some paperwork, but she also searched the internet for similar cases where artifacts were found on private property. Not surprisingly, she found quite a few, but none of them offered any promising resolutions. But she had no intention of giving up. She glanced at her watch. It was getting late and she had a stop to make before heading home.

Chapter 7

Sheri left her office and hurried across the street. She looked up at the Rantone Building as she approached. Named after her grandfather, an influential and very popular public figure, the building housed the offices of the city supervisors.

The idea of going to her former stepfather occurred to her earlier, but she decided against it. Now, she figured, why not give it a try? Nolan Chambers was the chairman of the city council. Surely he could do something to help. After all it was the council who initially gave Hamilton Development the green light to build the resort after they purchased the property. They confirmed and approved his blueprints and inspections, so perhaps he would help her get on the property and get samples to test. She definitely needed to ask him.

She got to the front door. It was a little after six, but she knew he'd still be in. He never left before seven o'clock. She signed in at the security desk and headed upstairs to Nolan's office. She knew most of the supervisors would be gone by now, but she hoped he'd still be there. She walked into the reception area of Nolan's office and looked around. No one was there, but she heard movement in the back office. "Hello?" she called out, seeing his office door still open and the lights on.

His assistant, Lori, came out of his office with a small watering can and a handful of dead leaves. "Hey, hi, Sheri," she said, surprised to see her there. "What are you doing here?"

Sheri had only been to her stepfather's office twice in the five years he and her mother had been married. Each time she'd been there to see her mother, but not this time. "Hi, Lori, I was hoping to catch Nolan before he went home. Is he still in the office?" she asked, noticing that the door was open and the lights were on.

"No, he's been in a meeting all day in Richmond."

"Do you know if he's coming back here or going home after Richmond?" Sheri asked.

"He's supposed to come back here later. At least

that's what he said. He called as he was waiting for the ferry to say he was on his way. That was about fifteen minutes ago."

Sheri looked at her watch. She knew she was better off trying to catch up with him here. "Do you mind if I wait for him?"

"No, help yourself," Lori said. "I'm headed out for the day." Sheri nodded and watched her water the small, nearly dying plant on her desk and then put the watering can on the floor under her desk. She turned off her desktop computer and grabbed her purse from the lower drawer. "Okay, I'm headed out. He shouldn't be too long getting here. As I said he called about fifteen minutes ago. If he's not here by the time you need to leave, just turn the latch on your way out. The door locks automatically."

"Okay, have a good weekend."

Sheri took a seat in the reception area as Lori came around to the front of the desk and grabbed her jacket from the peg behind the door. "You can wait in his private office if you want. But just do me a favor, don't touch his computer. He gets really pissed when people touch his computer."

"I won't," Sheri promised faithfully.

"See ya later."

"Okay, bye," Sheri said. A few minutes later Lori left and Sheri was sitting in the office alone with a stack of political magazines on the desk in front of her. She picked one up, flipped through it quickly and then placed it back exactly as she found it. There were a few brochures—Welcome to Crescent Island and See Our Growth—also on the desk. She grabbed one of each, opened them and looked through them. They were the typical tourism brochures she'd seen a dozen times before. The only difference was that these had a personal message from Nolan, the chairman of the board of supervisors.

He wrote about the beauty of the island and extolled its many treasures. It also went on to give his personal account of growing up here, which she thought was rather odd since he spent most of his life in Southern California. But that was Nolan. It was all about perception to him. He was a businessman, a politician and for the past three years her former stepfather.

When her father had died her mother was devastated. Having three young children to raise, she quickly remarried. It lasted two years. Sheri didn't even remember his name. Her mother remained single until she met Nolan. They fell in love and married. Nolan moved to the island and his political career blossomed. To his credit, Sheri believed he really had been in love with her mother.

She glanced up at the numerous awards, plaques and citations covering his walls. The office was like a shrine to Nolan's civic-mindedness. She stood, walked around and started reading a few. Noting the dates, most had been awarded within the past few years. It was obvious this was what Nolan treasured in life. Like her mother, appearances were everything to him. A person could be the most despicable being on the planet, but as long as they maintained a sense of propriety they were considered socially acceptable.

She opened the other brochure and saw all the projects the board of supervisors had planned for the future. There were several new cell phone towers, new stores and boutiques and, of course, expansion of the resort. It appeared that the quiet island she knew was all of a sudden changing. Recently she'd noticed that the outside world was beginning to corrupt the quaint little island that she loved so much. The evidence was all around her, coffee shop chains and fast-food restaurants were replacing the small-town, mom-and-pop businesses that once thrived in Crescent Island.

"Change," she whispered softly to herself. It seemed now everyone wanted a piece of the action. Land developers like Jordan Hamilton were carving up her hometown like a piece of pie. Each one took a bigger and bigger slice, leaving little or nothing for those who had cherished Crescent Island for decades.

She thought about the work site earlier today. The Hamilton Resort Complex was one of Nolan's new initiatives. She knew there would be more projects like them and more men like Jordan Hamilton. He was everything she despised about what was going on here. To him Crescent Island was just another sand pile to dig up, build his castle and move on. He came to make money and had no feeling and no connection to the island.

Her thoughts drifted to what she and Genie had talked about as they drove back to the museum. She had downplayed it, of course, but he really was gorgeous. Genie was right. The man exuded pure sex appeal. Everything about him screamed take me home and do me all night. A shiver shot through her as her stomach fluttered at the thought. She smiled as several uncharacteristic thoughts and images floated through her mind. Her mouth watered just thinking about him. She quickly caught herself. Maybe Genie was right. Maybe it had been too long.

Jordan parked his car and walked toward the city office building. He was feeling good—no, better than good. He cleverly avoided seeing Mamma Lou by asking Cleveland to go to Gates Manor and pick up the papers for Darius. Cleveland picked them up and delivered them to him with no problem. Jordan knew it was cowardly, but he did it anyway. Mamma Lou's matchmaking efforts had been avoided, and he was feeling fantastic.

He walked into the building, signed his name at

the security desk and then continued up to Nolan's office. He knew he had to fix this. But having politicians dictate to him what he could and couldn't do always irritated him. He looked at his watch as he opened the door and walked into the reception area. Lori, who was usually at her desk, wasn't there now. He looked around to see that Nolan's office door was open. He walked over and went in. The first thing he saw was a woman standing across the room staring at the wall.

Apparently she didn't hear him enter since she didn't turn around. He stood in the doorway watching silently as she examined one of the framed certificates on the wall. He wondered what could be so interesting. Then his gaze leisurely eased down her body and caressed the curvy silhouette of her body. He knew it wasn't Lori. Lori was much shorter and rounder and this woman, whoever she was, had the perfect shape for him. The roundness of her rear accentuated the slim, fitted skirt she wore. It stopped just above her knee, leaving much to his imagination. She had a narrow waist with long, luscious wraparound legs. No, this was definitely someone new. He smiled at the possibilities.

But oddly enough, after having many meetings with the supervisors over the past six to eight months, it was strange that he'd never seen her here before. Then he decided that perhaps she was new or maybe associated with another part of city government. He smiled. There was only one way to find out. "Good afternoon, I have an appointment with Nolan Chambers."

Sheri turned around. Her jaw dropped. Standing there in front of her was the man she'd just been fantasizing about. Her gaze dropped down the full length of his body. Clothes, body, face, everything was the same. Her eyes widened in surprise. It was like she had conjured him up out of thin air.

"You!"

His smile faded then broadened a split second later into what looked like utter pleasure.

"You," she repeated.

She watched as he walked casually into the room. His easy too-masculine swagger gave him an air of laid-back authority and homeboy arrogance. He stopped in the middle of the room and looked around. Apparently seeing that they were alone he continued toward her. She stood her ground.

"You know you have a way of saying that word and making it sound like I just stole your Halloween candy," he said.

He seemed a lot taller, broader, stronger and— heaven help her—sexier than she remembered. Whoa, where did that come from? A quick flash of heat shot through her body. Her mouth went dry and her stomach fluttered nonstop. Sexier, what was she thinking?

"What are you doing here?" she whispered

almost accusingly, hoping to quickly cool the hot lava surging through her body. He licked his lips. Her knees nearly buckled. Correction, what was she thinking with?

"I already answered that question. I have an appointment with Nolan this evening. What are you doing here?" he asked. "I thought you said you worked for the museum, that you were a curator."

"I said I was the museum's historian, not the curator."

"So what's the museum's historian doing here in the office of the chairman of the board of supervisors?" He paused a moment then realized the answer. "Don't tell me it's got something to do with that hole in the ground at the work site."

She glared at him without answering. He walked over and sat down on the arm of the sofa. The dynamics of their physical positions changed. Now they were nearly eye to eye. He'd had sunglasses on earlier, so this was the first time she actually saw his eyes. They were dark and dangerously sexy.

"So you're here to do what, somehow force me to allow you onto my property? Or do you intend to just shut me down?"

She moved closer to him standing at arm's length from him. "If you weren't so arrogant you'd see that a find of this magnitude could benefit both of us."

"Really, now how would shutting down my work site, putting over fifty hardworking men and woman out of work, delaying shipments and deliveries and pretty much costing me a small fortune benefit me?"

"I would never shut the whole work site down. I'm only interested in the small area on the side where the hole is located. There isn't much going on there anyway."

"At the moment, no there isn't. That's why I have the workers clearing that area, so that we can begin working."

"So, you are going to build something there."

He nodded. "That's the plan."

"It's a good thing plans can change."

"Not this time," he said quickly.

"We'll see," she snapped right back.

Jordan smiled again. He was beginning to like this. She had spirit. He liked that, too. "I suppose that means you intend to get the board of supervisors to renege on their contract with me." She didn't respond. He shook his head. "That's not how business works, sweetheart. But I am interested in one thing—what exactly do you expect to gain from all this?"

Sheri was instantly insulted but had no intention of being intimidated. "This isn't about personal gain, Mr. Hamilton. Not everybody has an agenda or blind ambition. And don't call me sweetheart."

"Yes, granted, I am ambitious. Most people are unless they're fooling themselves. I'm guessing you're ambitious as well. Otherwise, you wouldn't even be here. But the difference is my ambition doesn't get in the way of my ethics."

She felt his words sting. "If that's the case then you'll allow me to test the wood samples in the hole. That's all I'm asking. It's that simple."

"Take off the rose-colored glasses, Ms. Summers. Do you really think it's that simple? If there is something down there then the land could be seized and months of hard work and millions of dollars circles down the drain. Over fifty workers, dozens of vendors and subcontractors would have lost their jobs. So no, I can't allow that."

"You don't know that for sure and I can't imagine that would even happen."

He chuckled. "Let's just say I have firsthand knowledge and a lot of experience with situations like this. So trust me when I tell you, it's never that simple."

"It's only about that one space, not the whole property," she insisted. "It should be about what's right."

"Right for whom?" he asked quietly.

She immediately thought about the protective order her uncle would be signing Friday evening. She smiled. It was only a matter of time. By Monday she'd have her test samples. "You really don't get it, do you?"

"Look, I don't want to do this with you. Why

don't we call a truce and go grab a drink. I believe I still owe you one."

The man was infuriating. "Don't patronize me."

"I wouldn't think of it. You appear to be a very intelligent woman. I admire that."

Sheri shook her head in total exasperation. "I know what you admire and what you're doing."

"I beg your pardon?" he said.

"Yeah, you should beg my pardon."

"What exactly do I admire?" he asked innocently.

"You're trying to confuse the issue. It's not going to work. And don't think you're gonna sway me with your charm. That won't work, either, so save it."

He smiled happily even though he'd been found out. "I think I'm gonna enjoy sparring with you, Ms. Summers. Is it getting hot in here or is it just me?"

She stared directly into his dark sexy eyes. The man was cocky and brazen. He was also pushing her buttons and she was letting him. Apparently he was a lot better at this than she was. She took a deep breath. Her chest expanded. She watched his eyes gaze downward then back up into her eyes. His boyish smile was beyond seductive. "Don't," she said.

"Don't what."

"Don't even think about it."

"What?" he asked softly.

"You know what," she said, lowering her voice, as well.

Neither said anything for a few seconds. They were both feeling the intensity of the moment. And the way he was looking at her was making every nerve ending in her body quiver. She opened her mouth to speak, but no words came out. She took a cautious step back. "I think I need to go now." She turned to leave.

"One more thing, Ms. Summers," Jordan said.

"Yes?" Sheri turned back around. Then before she realized it, he had pulled her into his arms. She knew she needed to say something, do something. But her mind went completely blank. She was no fool. She knew what was going to happen next. She opened her mouth and in an instant his lips were on hers. He literally took her breath away. With her mouth already open, his tongue delved deep inside. She took all of him and then freely offered herself in return.

The kiss swept them up instantly, pressing deeper while connecting far more than just their mouths. Passions surged and lustful hunger prevailed. She heard him groan and the penetration of his tongue made her want more. She released her own deep throaty moan of pleasure. Her body ached to be closer. She felt his hand on her hips pulling her closer then they moved to her rear and pressed her between his legs. She felt the hardness of his arousal and got even more excited.

This was so wrong. She knew it, but she couldn't help herself. It was shameful. It was scandalous. But it was also so very, very addictive. At that very moment she wanted this. She wanted him. It had been a long time since a man made her feel so real and alive. No, she took it back. No man had ever made her feel like this before. She was on fire. Her mind became hazy. Her body seared with the intensity of her arousal. How could a kiss be this completely consuming? How could she be kissing this man? Where was her credibility? She needed to…

"Okay, okay," she said, then pushed back quickly as she tried to regain control over her wayward emotions. "No, I can't. We can't." Breathless, they just looked at each other. Neither spoke. If she didn't know any better she'd say he was just as surprised about the reaction to the kiss as she was. The passionate fire in their eyes was evident. They wanted more. He leaned in again. She leaned away, shook her head and stepped back. He released her slowly, reluctantly. "That was wrong," she said.

"Uh-uh, that felt right and you know it."

Yes, she knew it, but she'd never admit it to him. She also knew that if she didn't leave now, heaven knows what would happen. "Right or wrong, it won't happen again."

"Are you so sure about that?" he teased.

She looked at him sternly. The passion in his eyes went right through her. She nodded slowly. "I'm positive."

He simply smiled.

"Don't make the mistake of thinking you know me just because we kissed. You don't. I'm not one of your little groupies."

"I'm well aware of that," he said in barely a whisper.

They gazed into each other's eyes, each still sizing the other up. The way he looked at her made her churn inside. Her hormones were raging all through her body, but there was no way she was going to give in. It had been too long since she'd been in a man's arms. But it was her choice. She knew starting something with Jordan would lead to complications and she didn't need that. He was too tempting and she knew she needed to leave now. She took another step back. "Please think about what I said." She turned and walked to the office door.

"Sheri," he called out. She didn't turn around.

Jordan sat on the arm of the sofa and watched her leave. His smile broadened. He wanted to stop her and finish what they'd started, but he knew it was a bad idea. The last thing he needed was to get involved with someone here. This job was temporary. He'd be gone soon. He knew this wasn't going to be serious. He'd never allow it. Women didn't get close, he made sure of that. But right now getting close to Sheri was exactly what he wanted to do.

He licked his lips and then touched his mouth. The taste and feel of her was still with him and he was still wanting. He knew he could have any woman he wanted. But right now, there was only one he intended to get. She had started a fire in him that he knew only she could satisfy. He closed his eyes and shook his head. One kiss was all she gave him, but he knew it wasn't going to be enough.

He gazed across the room at the office door. Someone was coming. He thought Sheri was coming back to him. He stood waiting for her to come in. A few seconds later Nolan Chambers walked into his office and looked around to find Jordan staring at him. "Good, you're here. I was afraid I'd missed you. Traffic was crazy. Okay, let's get to it."

Jordan nodded slowly and watched Nolan walk behind his desk and drop his briefcase. He talked nonstop, but Jordan had no idea what he saying. Truthfully, he didn't really care. He was still thinking about the kiss. Twenty minutes later he got in his truck and just sat there. "Damn," he said aloud. "What was that?" Unbelieving, he shook his head. He didn't plan it and certainly hadn't expected it. It was just an impulse, something he never succumbed to.

Jordan eventually started his truck and drove

off. While still in town he decided to make a few stops. He had his truck washed and detailed, went to the local barbershop and then, on another whim, stopped at the local florist. Thoughts of Sheri kept running through his mind. He liked the feel of her against his body and he liked the taste of her in his mouth. He wondered what else he'd like.

It was nearly eight o'clock by the time he got to his condo rental. The meeting with Nolan had taken much longer than he'd expected. He grabbed his briefcase and went inside. He turned on the light and looked around. Monochromatic colors, bland, uninteresting furniture and a weighty emptiness greeted him at the door. Maybe this was why he preferred to work late. But in all honesty, it was the same thing at home in Virginia.

He had bought and renovated an old country farmhouse a few years ago. It was something he always wanted to do. He soon realized it was the journey and challenge of the renovation and not necessarily the end result that appealed him. It was the same with the women in his life. He enjoyed the chase. Once caught, he soon lost interest in them.

He went into the kitchen, grabbed a bottle of water and then headed out onto the balcony. He thought about the kiss. It was nice. He wondered about Sheri. He didn't know a lot about her, just what little he'd read on the internet. He looked out over the vast landscape, knowing she lived out there someplace.

Sheri was so upset she could hardly contain herself. She hurried back across the street to the museum. When she got to her office she sat down at her desk and closed her eyes. She started thinking about all the things she should have said and done, but didn't. But what she was really thinking about was the kiss. It was explosive. It was obvious that hunger had ravaged them. They both needed the release.

He had wrapped his arms around her waist as his hand held the nape of her neck in place to deepen their connection. His hand had drifted down to her blouse. He had gently squeezed her breast. Her nipples hardened instantly. She had felt his thumb brush across the tender nib. She closed her eyes as her mind shattered in a million different directions.

An hour and a half later she glanced up at the clock and saw that it was really late. She packed up her briefcase and left hoping tomorrow would be better.

Chapter 8

Tomorrow wasn't better. And neither was the next day or the day after that or the day after that. She hadn't heard from Hamilton and she was quickly losing patience. If he had found something on-site he wasn't telling her. Jack was just as bad, although he did send her an email telling her that he had contacted the Hamilton Development Corporation and they would be looking into it. In other words nothing was being done and she was running out of time.

By Thursday after work Sheri decided to take matters into her own hands. She knew she couldn't just let it go. This was too important and Jack was obviously going to be of no help. So, instead of going home she drove in the opposite direction and headed to Crescent Point. She needed to talk to Jordan Hamilton once more. She hoped that if she were composed and laid her argument out calmly, he'd listen to her. He had to. There's no way he could be the coldhearted arrogant jerk Genie's boyfriend claimed he was. But given their first meeting, he just might be. Still she had to try.

As she neared the construction site her heart trembled. She drove up the street noticing that the cars and trucks she'd seen earlier were all gone. It was late. It hadn't occurred to her that he might not still be there. She parked close, got out and walked to the front gate. The security guard she remembered from earlier was still there. He walked up and greeted her. "Good evening, welcome back," he said, smiling evenly.

The insincerity of the expression on his face betrayed nothing. She nodded. "Good evening. Is Mr. Hamilton still here?"

"Let me check," he said, pulling out his cell phone. After a brief conversation he requested that she follow him. He escorted her to the same trailer she had been in before. As they walked up the steps Jordan Hamilton opened the door.

"Good evening, Ms. Summers," he said cordially as he stepped outside onto the small deck.

He nodded to Cleveland, who immediately turned and walked away.

He was dressed in dark blue jeans and a white polo shirt. Her heart nearly sputtered upon seeing him. He'd shaved. He looked young, clean-cut and handsome. She wasn't sure if she preferred the rugged construction-worker look or this suave, sexy look. Either way Genie was right, he was gorgeous. He extended his hand to shake. She looked down at his hand, but didn't oblige. "I won't bite, I promise," he said, joking lightheartedly.

She immediately looked up, completely embarrassed. "Oh, no, I mean, I'm sorry. I didn't mean to imply…"

"I'm joking, I'm joking," he said calmingly, but realizing that she still hadn't shaken his hand.

For the first time she noticed that he had smiled and it was radiant. "I don't…" she began.

"Shake hands?" he guessed. "I understand. My friend and attorney doesn't, either, he's a germaphobe."

"I'm not a germaphobe, I just…" She stopped, realizing how crazy she was going to sound if she told him the truth. She didn't shake hands because she was afraid she had the same gift her grandmother had. "It's a long story, a personal thing. No offense."

"None taken," he said quietly.

She noted the soft tenderness in his voice. She

took a deep breath and resolved that she was determined not to get distracted or lose her temper. "Mr. Hamilton, in our last conversation, you assured me…" she began.

"Perhaps we can start again and this time, dispense with the formalities. My name is Jordan."

She nodded. "Sheri," she said.

"Sheri, that's a beautiful name."

"Thank you, Jordan."

"Sheri, about the last time we were together…" he said.

"I think it would be best if we just forget about what happened between us. We were both excited about what's at stake. The moment got out of hand. So, given that," she said in one breath, "I think we need to talk and come to some kind of better understanding."

"I see," he said as he walked over to the wooden rail and looked up at the evening sky. "Then I'm afraid you came back for no reason. My position hasn't changed," he said firmly.

"I just need a few minutes."

He paused a moment, seemingly trying to decide whether to agree to her request. Then he nodded and relented. "Come on inside." He opened the door and stepped aside as she walked in. Soft soul music played quietly in the background. She recognized the group. It was En Vogue. "Have a seat, please."

"No, thank you," she said.

"Can I get you something? Water, coffee, tea?"

"No, I'm fine, thanks. This isn't a social call," she said firmly then walked over to the large slanted drawing table and looked down at the plans, then back up at him. "I know you're busy, so I'll be brief. I feel we need to come to an—"

"Understanding," he said, finishing her statement. She nodded. "But in this case I don't see that an understanding is necessarily needed. You've stated your position. I've stated mine. Since what you want is on my property and directly opposed to my interests, there's no discussion."

"I don't understand how you can say that. You've obviously come to this island because of what we have here and who we are. Well, what might be in that hole is the beginning of who we are. The importance of knowing that is critical."

"To you, yes. But not to me. I have a timetable I need to keep. That's critical to me."

"One more building more or less isn't going to change anything. As a matter of fact, less is better. Why be so intent on changing us?"

"That's it, isn't it? Change. Lady, history is only for schoolbooks. You're opposed to change."

"No," she said too quickly, and then reversed herself. "Yes. But not for the reasons you think. You're right. I think Crescent Island is beautiful. It's perfect just as it is. We don't need big developers to come here and change us into something we're not. I look out my window at the museum and see everything I once knew and everything that was charming about this island turning into a strip mall. That's your change."

"We're not trying to change the island."

"Then what do you call all this?" she said, looking around. "This is change."

"As a historian I suppose you want this place to be forever frozen in time. Life doesn't work that way. Time moves on. Things do change whether you want them to or not. There's a reason people don't live in huts or thatched-roof houses anymore, or dress in animal skins. Change happens for the good."

"Not always. We don't need all this stuff."

"Perhaps you'd prefer us to live in some other time."

"I didn't say that," she snapped, then watched the corner of his mouth tip slightly into a smile.

"It was implied," he said. His voice was low and sexy.

"How did we get off the subject? I didn't come here to talk about real estate development. I came here to talk to you about the artifacts that were found."

He shook his head. "Repeatedly calling them artifacts isn't going to make a hole in the ground and a bunch of wood any more important."

"You know, if I didn't know any better, I'd say you were enjoying this," she whispered.

"Aren't you?" he said just as quietly.

"No," she said too quickly. She watched the corner of his lips tip upward even more. "No," she repeated for emphasis.

"Then I guess it's a good thing you know better," he said.

They stared at each other a moment until Sheri looked away. The deep penetrating look in his eyes unnerved her. There was more behind every word he spoke, as if he knew something she didn't. Everything seemed to have a different meaning. They didn't know each other, but the sense of something more profound was undeniable. "I was wondering when you were going to show up. Tell me, are you always this angry or is it just me?" he said.

"Surprisingly, only around you," she said.

"Yeah, well, you'd be surprised how many people say that."

"Actually, I wouldn't," she replied, but refused to smile even though he chuckled at her response. She suppressed it then gave in to the burning feeling of a grin pulling her lips wide.

"Aw, look, so you do know how to loosen up and smile."

"I'm not some stiff-lipped old maid."

"That's good to know."

She tilted her head and looked at him intently.

She squinted her eyes as if to see beyond the facade. "What exactly do you want, Mr. Hamilton?"

"I think that's a question I should be asking you."

"I'm not doing this for me. It's not personal. It's the history of this island that's going to die if I don't do anything about it. I don't have a choice. I can't let that happen."

"Neither will I," he said almost too calmly.

"Let me make something very clear to you— your charms don't work on me. I just want to take some tests and that's it."

"What kinds of tests exactly?"

"Primarily radiocarbon dating tests."

"How long?"

"That depends."

"On what?"

"On what we find down there."

"There's nothing down there."

Before she responded, the office phone rang. "Excuse me, I've been expecting a call this evening," he said, then walked over to the desk and picked it up.

"Sure, of course," she said. She needed a break from their conversation, which was going nowhere. She knew he was deliberately trying to get to her. She watched as he picked up the receiver and began talking. Instead of sitting, she got up and looked around the trailer studying the sketches, the framed architectural drawings on the walls and the design plans on the drafting board. One in particular got her attention. She paused in front and examined it more closely. A few moments later Jordan hung up and walked over. She turned to him as he approached.

"Who was your architect on this project?"

"Me, I'm the architect."

"You," she said, more than a little astonished.

He chuckled again. "Yes, me," he said. "Now why should that surprise you so much? I'm not just a pretty face."

"I wasn't surprised—" she said awkwardly. He looked at her with a half smile, knowing she wasn't being truthful. She tried not to smile, knowing that he knew she was lying. "Much," she added, feeling her cheeks burn hotly. "Did you always want to be an architect?"

"Me, nah. When I was a child I wanted to be an artist. I painted, sculpted and sketched everything in sight."

"Really? That's interesting," she said in astonishment.

"Oh, yeah, I went to school for architecture and even worked in a top firm for a few years."

"Then you just stopped, just like that."

"Yes, we all did. I was an architect, Darius was a stockbroker and Julian was a doctor in Boston."

"What? How? Why?"

"Our dad owned a small construction company when we were growing up. He and our mom divorced and he bent over backward to give us everything. He got sick and died. We didn't want to see his dream disappear so we changed careers and took over the business."

"That's so wonderful. I can see you loved him very much."

"Yes, very much."

Their eyes connected and the warmth she felt on her face swept lower. Still, she refused to look away from the intensity of his gaze. She took a deep breath to steady her nerves. There was something about this man that did things to her, unsettling things. She began feeling the turbulence of anticipation stir inside of her. Something was coming. He took a step even closer to stand right behind her. He was too close. The muscles in his forearm tensed. He seemed to exude raw power without even trying.

He turned to look at the framed drawing on the wall and spoke. She closed her eyes and inhaled deeply. His spicy cologne filled her lungs and the warmth she felt on her cheeks was now a sultry burn all over her body. All of the sudden it had gotten hot in the trailer. Everything seemed to move in slow motion. He talked, but there was no way she was listening to what he was saying.

Her mouth went dry and all she could think about was touching him, but not to shake his hand. She was way past that. She wanted to really touch him, to feel him, to have him touch and feel her. She wanted to know what it was like to have him hold her in his arms again. To feel the solid hard strength of his body pressed to hers once more. She looked up at his mouth as he talked. His lips were perfect. She wanted them on her.

When he turned back to her, she quickly averted her eyes to look at the drawings on the wall. She needed to distract herself fast. But it was too late.

"Are you okay?" he asked. "You look a little flush."

"I'm fine," she lied again. She knew her reaction to him was too obvious and he had to know he was unnerving her. She moved away to the next rendering knowing he was watching her now. She could feel his dark, penetrating eyes as they burned all over her body. "These are all very beautiful. You're very talented. They're incredibly innovative," she finally managed to utter in a faint voice.

"Thank you," he said, stepping to stand right beside her again. Too close. She eased away to the other side of the drawing table hoping he wouldn't follow. He did and unfortunately she was blocked in. There was no retreating from the space behind the drafting table. She had to go around him to get out. "I'm glad you like them," he said, leaning back on the raised surface.

"So, you're an artist," she said as casually as she could.

"Sometimes, yes," he agreed.

She shook her head to clear the last of her stray thoughts. "Then I don't understand, how…?"

He held his hand up. "Allow me, how can I draw and create designs so imaginative and beautiful and not appreciates the museum's stance and the importance of what you want."

"Exactly."

"I appreciate your position, I just don't agree with it. It's business, not personal."

"It's personal for me."

"Yeah, I get that. Your passion is…" he began then paused.

"Lacking?" she suggested, having heard it from Jack.

"No way, definitely not, your passion is evident. You're excited about your work. I knew that the second I saw and heard you going off on Leroy. Which, by the way, takes a lot of nerve. He's six foot six and weights nearly three hundred and fifty pounds."

She smiled and felt relaxed. "I see your point. It never occurred to me to be concerned. I guess I should have been."

"What, about Leroy? No, you shouldn't. He's a great guy. He's really a marshmallow."

"I have a feeling you'd probably say that about all the people who work for you."

"Most of them anyway," he confirmed.

"So, Hamilton Development Corporation, you're one big happy family," she said.

"I wouldn't say all that. Sometimes we are, sometimes not. No matter what, there's always somebody in charge."

"And I think you like being in charge, don't you?"

He smiled seductively. Her insides twisted. "Not always. Sometimes I like to be submissive."

"No kidding," she said drily.

"You have drive. I admire that in you. I like it. It's refreshing. That's something I've been struggling with lately. Tell me, are you this passionate about everything in your life?"

"Everything?" she questioned. He didn't reply. He knew she knew exactly what he was suggesting. He smiled again. Her insides turned into mush. "Yes," she said on a whim.

"Good, I'm glad to hear that," he said. She blushed and looked away. "I've been trying to figure you out since we met."

She looked surprised. "Why would you want to try and figure me out?"

"Because you're puzzling, because you're beautiful and because you're not the same woman I met several months ago." She turned to look at him. "Yeah, I remember you very well. Shy, reserved, quiet."

She took a deep breath and watched him as he moved closer. "And now this week you march out here on my property and confront a man sitting behind a bulldozer like it was an everyday occurrence. Then when he starts the engine, you jump right in front of it to protect something you're not even sure is down there. Why? For history's sake?"

"You asked and answered your own question. You're an architect. You must see the beauty of the buildings that were created before you."

"Yes, but I also see the flaws," he said

"You see flaws, I see character. The history of a building, flaws and all, holds its spirit and its heart. It's where we get our sense of…" She paused, seeing the broad smile on his face. "Sorry, I guess I'm getting carried away."

"I think I like it when you get carried away. You should do it more often."

"Now you're being facetious."

"No, I'm not, you really are amazing."

"History isn't just about what we read in books. It's everything around us and everyone that came before us. There's a connection that's unbreakable. We learn from history and Crescent Island has so much of it to share. Have you ever actually taken the time to experience it?"

"What do you mean?"

"Have you actually seen the island, experienced the natural beauty and scenic places?" she asked. He shook his head. "Maybe you should."

"Yeah, maybe I should." The look in his eyes stilled her.

"What?" she asked as he stared at her.

"I've been trying to think what is it about you that has been drawing us together?"

"Drawing us together?" she repeated shaking her head. "I don't know what you're talking about," she lied. She felt it and now she knew he felt it, too. It was an attraction that she'd never experienced so strongly before. They were like magnets being drawn together. The more they tried to resist, the more powerful the attraction.

He nodded and then walked around to the front of the drafting table where she stood. "I think you do," he said. "I think you know exactly what I'm talking about, don't you, Sheri?" He stopped and stood right in front of her. She looked up as he licked his lips. The lips she wanted all over her body just a few minutes ago. Now, pushing those thoughts aside was impossible. It was like a dam had cracked and the forces of desire had been released. She felt the gravity of the moment taking over. They were single. They were adults. They were here together. A second later they were consumed by an explosive kiss.

She kissed him. It came swiftly without warning when it happened. It was impulsive and passionate, in a moment of reckless abandon. The feeling overwhelmed them as the urgency to release their sexual tension took over. They surrendered willingly to the passion that seized them.

Jordan pressed his tongue to her lips. She parted her lips and opened up to him. His tongue delved into her mouth and playfully intertwined in rapturous delight. Then the kiss slowed. They began nibbling, pecking and tasting one another as the momentum increased to a feverish pitch.

She wrapped her arms around his neck as he pulled her waist closer to his body. She leaned in to him. He held her tight as they resumed their kiss. This time it was filled with breathless desire.

He turned and pressed her back against the angled surface of the drafting table. She felt the thick hardness of his erection bear down against her thighs. The sensation was overwhelming. Her insides trembled. All her senses short-circuited and every nerve ending in her body tingled. She was on fire, and feeling the hardness of his body was like pouring accelerant on a blazing fire. He ran his hands down her body, over her shoulders, to her breasts, to her stomach, then her hips, then to her thighs. Just as he grabbed hold of the hem of her skirt and pulled it up, the phone rang.

Startled, she stood rooted in place. Seconds later, she pushed back and eased away as he leaned back and released her. Breathless, she closed her eyes, turned and walked away as Jordan's phone rang a second time. She was flustered and needed to get her body under control. She wanted him and if they hadn't been interrupted, who knows what would have happened after a few more minutes. "No," she said aloud, more to herself. "I can't. I'm sorry. I can't believe I just did that."

"Sheri," Jordan said softly, walking over to stand behind her. "I'm not complaining. As a matter of fact…"

"It was unprofessional. I shouldn't have come here tonight," she chided herself. Jordan took her hand. She immediately felt it. It was like a bolt of lightning shooting through her body. It was exactly the way her grandmother always said it would be. "No, this was a huge mistake."

"No, it wasn't," he said, drawing her close again. He placed his hands on her shoulders and pulled her back against his body. He leaned down to nuzzle her ear. "What happened was natural. It probably would have happened months ago if…"

She shook her head. "I have to go."

He relaxed his hold and eased her around to face him. He tipped her chin upward, leaned down and kissed her forehead, her eyelids, her cheeks and the underside of her chin. "Sheri, you want me as much as I want you. Why are you fighting this?"

Her stomach jumped. He did it again. He threw her off guard. "Good night, Jordan," she said.

"Sheri, are you sure you want to leave?" he asked softly. "Right now you want me as much as I want you."

"Wanting something or someone doesn't make it right."

"Why not?" he asked, moving closer to her. "What if it's too right?"

Sheri swallowed hard. He was right. She did want him. Every nerve ending in her body screamed out to touch him, feel him and be with him. But she was more than a sexual animal. She grabbed her purse just as he touched her arm. He stroked the length of her arm to her hand. Their fingers intertwined. He moved closer. The space between them vanished. He dipped his head down to the curve of her neck and nuzzled her tenderly. Then he kissed her earlobe, her cheek and the sweet curve of her neck. She took in a quick breath as her body burned inside.

His other hand came up to her hip then over to her stomach, holding her in place. His fingers spread wide. She gasped as she felt the hardness of his erection behind her. She closed her eyes. "Are you sure you want to leave me?" he whispered.

"We can't do this," she mumbled slowly.

"Yes, we can," he said as he turned her around slowly and tipped her chin up to his. "I want to make love to you tonight. Right here, right now. I need to feel all of you—stay with me. You can't keep pretending this isn't happening between us."

"Jordan…"

"You want to walk out that door, fine. But ask yourself, what if?" He kissed her neck. "So, what's it gonna be, Sheri. Do you want to lose control tonight?"

She closed her eyes and took a deep breath as the heat of the moment took over. It was all suddenly so crystal clear. Right now, this second, she wanted him more than anything else in the world. She reached up and wrapped her arms around his neck. She wanted this. She needed this. "Yes."

Chapter 9

Instantly their desire exploded as they rode the waves of passion. A barrage of kisses erupted from his lips. Arms caressed, tongues entwined, lips parted easily. A mindless procession of passion surged. There was hunger and longing and desire all coming at them at once. Weak and breathless, the cravings of long past denials ruptured. His hands caressed her everywhere and she loved it. Then, as if to conserve their passion for later, they slowed to tender nibbles and intimate touches.

She felt his hardness through his jeans. Hearing him groan his pleasure, she stroked him again. She unbuckled his belt and pulled it free. She pushed him back, getting his undivided attention. His eyes darkened even more if that was possible. Confused, he stared at her. She smiled teasingly as she reached out and touched his shoulder. She stroked down the length of his arm as she moved to circle around him.

When she got to his back she looked down at the sweet perfection of his butt, anticipating seeing a lot more of it. She ran her hands across his shoulders down his back to his rear then circled around to the other side of him. He stared at her as she stood in front of him again. "Nice," she said admiringly.

He nodded, looking down the length of her body. "Oh, yes, I totally agree."

She grabbed his shirt and pulled it out of the waistband of his jeans tossing it to the side. Good Lord. Her heartbeat nearly faltered at the sight of him. His chest was pure magnificence, smooth, brown and stunning. She nodded. "Very nice."

He reached out to her blouse and began unbuttoning the front. When the last button was free, he opened it and smiled as he took in the sweet swell of her breasts swollen under her lace bra. He licked his lips. "Oh, yes, very nice indeed." He unsnapped the front clasp, freeing her breasts. His eyes quickly glazed over and his jaw dropped. "Oh, yes." His mouth connected. She gasped when his tongue licked and tickled her nipple and he pinched the other. She pulled back, but with his hand on her hip, he held her in place.

"Jordan," she moaned. "Jordan," she gasped louder.

He licked and suckled hard, drawing her farther into the warmth of his mouth. He encircled her waist and drew her closer. Then he picked her up and carried her to the private room in the back of the trailer. He sat down on the bed with her on his lap. She slid off his lap, stood and pulled him up. She reached to the side and unzipped her skirt. He unzipped his pants. Her skirt fell, his jeans dropped. He stood in his boxer briefs and she in her lace panties.

He rimmed his finger around the waistband, then pulled her panties down as he dropped his briefs to the floor. He kissed her waist, stomach, her hips and her thighs. He stroked her body, sending shock wave after shock wave through her. She held tight to his shoulders as he feasted on her. "Wait, do you have condoms?"

"Yeah," he said, then grabbed his jeans pulling a condom from his wallet. He covered himself as she lay back on the bed. She reached out to beckon him. He came to her, hovered and then began kissing every inch of her body. She burned, anticipating what he'd do to her next. Hands, lips and tongue, he touched her, stroked her, caressed her, sending her body into arousal overload. He dipped his body between her legs. She bent her knees and wrapped her legs around him. His penis touched her opening. She reached down and stroked the long thickness. He throbbed, pulsating with liquid fire.

"Yes," she moaned. "Come inside."

He did. Pressing slow and steadily, he delved deep into her tightness all at once. She grabbed his forearms and held tight. Her body arched as he deepened his penetration. He got to his knees inching her rear up off the bed. He withdrew and then thrust inside again. The fluidness of his movements was meant for her. He hit her G-spot every time. She never knew so much tension could build up inside. Each thrust relaxed her body even more. Holding back became almost impossible. She gasped repeatedly, louder and louder. He was methodical. She closed her eyes as she felt his deep penetration.

"No, open your eyes. I want to see you come for me." It was hard, nearly impossible, but she did it. She watched as he watched her. The intensity in his eyes grew each time her plunged into her.

Then she released. She held her breath as the mounting climax came. She stiffened and then let go. He didn't stop. He plunged again. She climaxed again and again. She looked up at him, seeing his restraint had weakened. She wrapped her arms around his neck. He sat up, positioning her so that they were eye to eye. Connected, she sat straddling his hips and began pressing her body to his. They kissed then she leaned back and he captured her breast. He rocked his body faster and faster.

She watched, knowing he was coming. Then he stopped and lay back, bringing her on top of him. He bucked into her. She rode him until it was nearly impossible to stay on. He grabbed her hips one last time then he exploded. His body jerked and tensed then jerked again. She pressed into him again, tensing her inner muscles and feeling his hardness one last time. He looked up at her and released. Breathless, she lay down on top of his body. He wrapped his arms around her. Neither spoke. They were still too stunned by their explosive lovemaking. She'd never experienced anything like it. She did things she'd never thought of before, but it seemed so right with him.

Soon their breathing returned to normal. He continued to stroke her back and massage her rear. "I'm sure there are some appropriate words to describe this moment," she said.

He chuckled, making her body ripple with his. "If there are, I have no idea what they would be. Maybe there's a card."

She laughed this time and slowly got up. She looked around the room and saw an adjacent bathroom. She grabbed her clothes, went in and closed the door. When she came out five minutes later he

An Important Message from the Publisher

Dear Reader,

Because you've chosen to read one of our fine novels, I'd like to say "thank you"! And, as a special way to say thank you, I'm offering to send you two more Kimani™ Romance novels and two surprise gifts—absolutely FREE! These books will keep it real with true-to-life African American characters that turn up the heat and sizzle with passion.

Please enjoy the free books and gifts with our compliments...

Glenda Howard
For Kimani Press™

Peel off Seal and Place Inside...

FREE GIFTS SEAL

W e'd like to send you two free books to introduce you to Kimani™ Romance books. These novels feature strong, sexy women, and African-American heroes that are charming, loving and true. Our authors fill each page with exceptional dialogue, exciting plot twists, and enough sizzling romance to keep you riveted until the very end!

KIMANI ROMANCE...LOVE'S ULTIMATE DESTINATION

Your two books have combined cover price of $12.50 in the U.S. $14.50 in Canada, but are yours **FREE!**

We'll even send you two wonderful surprise gifts. You can't lose!

2 FREE BONUS GIFTS!

We'll send you two wonderful surprise gifts, (worth about $10) absolutely FREE just for giving KIMANI™ ROMANCE books a try! Don't miss out—MAIL THE REPLY CARD TODAY!

Visit us online at www.ReaderService.com

THE EDITOR'S "THANK YOU" FREE GIFTS INCLUDE:

➤ Two Kimani™ Romance Novels
➤ Two exciting surprise gifts

YES! I have placed my Editor's "thank you" Free Gifts seal in the space provided at right. Please send me 2 FREE Books, and my 2 FREE Mystery Gifts. I understand that I am under no obligation to purchase anything further, as explained on the back of this card.

PLACE
FREE GIFTS
SEAL
HERE

168/368 XDL FJKD

Please Print

FIRST NAME

LAST NAME

ADDRESS

APT.#

CITY

STATE/PROV.

ZIP/POSTAL CODE

Thank You!

Offer limited to one per household and not applicable to series that subscriber is currently receiving.

Your Privacy—The Reader Service is committed to protecting your privacy. Our Privacy Policy is available online at www.ReaderService.com or upon request from the Reader Service. We make a portion of our mailing list available to reputable third parties that offer products we believe may interest you. If you prefer that we not exchange your name with third parties, or if you wish to clarify or modify your communication preferences, please visit us at www.ReaderService.com/consumerchoice or write to us at Reader Service Preference Service, P.O. Box 9062, Buffalo, NY 14269. Include your complete name and address.

▶ Detach card and mail today. No stamp needed. ▶

© 2011 HARLEQUIN ENTERPRISES LIMITED ™ and ™ are trademarks owned and used by the trademark owner and/or its licensee. Printed in the U.S.A.

K-ROM-11C

The Reader Service - Here's How It Works:

Accepting your 2 free books and 2 free gifts (gifts valued at approximately $10.00) places you under no obligation to buy anything. You may keep the books and gifts and return the shipping statement marked "cancel." If you do not cancel, about a month later we'll send you 4 additional books and bill you just $4.94 each in the U.S. or $5.49 each in Canada. That is a savings of at least 21% off the cover price. Shipping and handling is just 50¢ per book in the U.S. and 75¢ per book in Canada.* You may cancel at any time, but if you choose to continue, every month we'll send you 4 more books, which you may either purchase at the discount price or return to us and cancel your subscription.
*Terms and prices subject to change without notice. Prices do not include applicable taxes. Sales tax applicable in N.Y. Canadian residents will be charged applicable taxes. Offer not valid in Quebec. All orders subject to credit approval. Credit or debit balances in a customer's account(s) may be offset by any other outstanding balance owed by or to the customer. Offer available while quantities last. Books received may not be as shown. Please allow 4 to 6 weeks for delivery.

If offer card is missing write to: The Reader Service, P.O. Box 1867, Buffalo, NY 14240-1867 or visit www.ReaderService.com

BUSINESS REPLY MAIL
FIRST-CLASS MAIL   PERMIT NO. 717   BUFFALO, NY

POSTAGE WILL BE PAID BY ADDRESSEE

THE READER SERVICE
PO BOX 1867
BUFFALO NY 14240-9952

NO POSTAGE
NECESSARY
IF MAILED
IN THE
UNITED STATES

was back in his jeans, with his shirt still open, sitting on the side of the bed.

Seeing her, he smiled. "You are beautiful." He reached out to her. She came, fitting between his legs. He looked up. "You're an amazing woman."

"Thank you. I think I'd better go," she said, noticing the sadness in his eyes.

"Can I see you tomorrow? We can have dinner."

She shook her head slowly. "That's probably not a good idea. This is already complicated. It's business, not personal. You said so yourself."

"I can separate the two, can you?" He leaned up and kissed her slowly, letting his tongue linger to taste the sweetness of her lips. "Let it go, Sheri. Trust me, you won't win this," he said.

She stepped back seeing the self-assuredness in his eyes. It was the same expression she remembered from before. "Don't suppose you know me just because we made love. You don't. Yes, I can separate business from the personal. I will win and you will stop the construction on that site."

"You think so," he challenged.

"I know so," she assured him.

"I love a challenge."

"It isn't a challenge, Jordan. It's a promise." She walked back into the office area and looked around for her purse.

"Then I guess we'll just have to wait and see.

But I do have one question. What if we both walked away too soon the last time?"

"Good night, Jordan." She grabbed her purse and quickly left the trailer. She got in her car and drove straight to her condo with all the windows rolled down. A breeze blew across her face. She went over what had transpired again and again in her head. She was trying to figure out what happened. When did everything change? Okay, she knew what happened. They made love and it was good, too damn good. Good Lord, her body ached now just thinking about it. The feel of his hands on her rear pulling her toward his hardness had her twitching.

The whole way home she couldn't stop thinking about what happened. She didn't know if he was playing her or not. It was possible. The last time they were together there was no way he was even remotely interested in her. Now everything seemed so different. But still, it wasn't as if she had feelings for him. She couldn't. How could she?

At home she showered and crawled into bed with her laptop, hoping that her usual routine would quell her raging hormones. It didn't. Eventually curiosity got the best of her and she typed Jordan's name into the search engine. A number of sites appeared. She opened a few and peered at the man she was just with. He was an architect and contractor and so much more.

By eleven o'clock she'd pushed the laptop aside

and lay with her back against the pillow staring up at the ceiling. She closed her eyes and thought about Jordan making love to her. She licked her lips, but his taste was long gone. She reached up and touched her mouth and then her breasts. The feel of him was still there. The closeness and fire still raged in her body. She wanted more. But what really upset her was that she'd lied to herself. She did have feelings for him. They were dangerous feelings that would only break her heart in the end. He was tempting. He'd caught her off guard once, but that wouldn't happen again. She'd make sure of that.

Moments later she heard thunder in the distance as the light patter of rain pelted her window. She rolled over. Closed her eyes and drifted off to sleep with Jordan's parting words echoing in her mind. *What if we both walked away too soon the last time?*

"Yeah, what if," she muttered before sleep overtook her.

Chapter 10

Jordan watched her leave. He considered going after her, but knew it would be a mistake for both of them. Instead, he gathered up his things, locked the office and headed out. Cleveland was coming toward the trailer just as he locked the door. "Good night, Cleveland."

"Jordan, I was just coming to get you, got a minute?"

"Sure, what's up?"

"I think you might want to see this."

Jordan walked with Cleveland to the secondary site. It was obvious even in the darkness that someone had been there. The ground around the area was dug up in several places and one of the other security guards was carefully putting a metal flashlight into a Ziploc bag. "Did you find anybody?"

"No, just the flashlight. The battery was dead," Cleveland said. "Whoever did this was unprepared this time."

Jordan shook his head. "Close the circle on this."

Cleveland nodded his head to the other security guard.

Jordan turned and headed back to the front of the site.

"Whoever did this knows exactly what they're doing and what's going on up here," said Cleveland. "They're looking for something and I don't think they found it, which means they'll be back. And we'll be ready. I suggest we install some surveillance cameras along the back fence over there. It looks like that was the point of entry."

Jordan nodded. Cleveland was the best of the best when it came to security. He intended to leave everything up to him. "I'll talk to Ian and Tamika tomorrow. I want you to get whatever you need to finish this. Put it in yourself. I want this done quietly, just the four of us."

Cleveland nodded. "Understood. I'll take care of it."

Jordan went back to the office, picked up a box and closed the office door behind him. Maybe he would do as Ian suggested and take the weekend off. It was something he hadn't done in a long time. Maybe a little R & R was just what he needed. He locked the door, waved to the security guards and headed to his truck. He put the box on the passenger seat and took off for the night.

He caught the last ferry off the island that evening. On the way back to the mainland he usually made calls or followed up on emails during the twenty-minute boat ride across the bay, but tonight his mood was introspective.

Making love to Sheri Summers was a calculated move. He had decided to catch her off guard. He succeeded. What he hadn't expected was to feel the way he felt afterward. He wanted more. He liked the way she tasted and felt in his arms. Women were usually putty in his hands. A little charm and charisma and he could get them to do whatever he wanted, whenever he wanted. He needed to find a way to charm Sheri. If she made a big deal about this, his plan would have failed and he had no intention of letting that happen.

He thought about the first night he met Sheri at Mamma Lou's house months ago. He had liked her instantly and that was the problem. It was an obvious setup and he refused to be manipulated like a pawn in a chess game and yield to Mamma Lou's matchmaking. So he dismissed her without giving her a chance. He knew he had hurt her feelings, and he regretted it. Now he wasn't sure if this was more

about that moment than her desire to claim some
artifacts that he wasn't sure were even there.

He stood out on the deck of the ferry, leaned
on the railing and looked out into the darkness as
the boat cut through the water. The clouds were
heavy and a thin veil of moisture hung in the air.
The sound of thunder rolled in the distance and his
thoughts seemed to roll with them. He knew Aunt
Ellen and Mamma Lou both had his best interests
at heart. They just didn't understand. What was so
wrong with being single? A thought immediately
popped into his head. What was so right?

As soon as the ferry docked he got off and
headed to his car. He often drove Interstate 95 like
it was his own personal autobahn. Tonight was no
exception. He zipped in and out of traffic with the
skill of a Formula 1 driver. Thankfully the high-
way was nearly empty. It wasn't the fact that he was
running late that pushed him so hard tonight. It was
thinking about Sheri. Something happened between
them. He felt it and he knew she felt it, too.

Admitting that he liked her when he saw her
months ago was easy. He did. What red-blooded
man wouldn't? Sheri was beautiful, intelligent and
passionate. She had a perfect body with just right
curves to make a man drool, a stunning face and
she exuded enough sexual appeal to have a man
walking sideways for weeks. But it was her unas-
suming nature, her innocence that got him. She was

a woman that needed to have a man by her side, but it wouldn't be him.

He liked his freedom and enjoyed his lifestyle just the way it was. The women he usually dated were glamorous businesswomen who worked around-the-clock like he did. Their relationships had been mainly physical with little or no emotional attachment. In the past two years he had dated a CEO, a doctor, a lawyer and a model. They all fit perfectly into his well-ordered life. As soon as one got too clingy he broke it off. He was never in any danger of falling in love. Things never got serious. He made sure of that.

He smiled. He had certainly thought about Sheri from time to time, but never contacted her. But now, after their sexual tryst, he couldn't stop thinking about her. The kiss they shared had started a fire burning inside of him. And this time, he wasn't willing to walk away. He wanted more.

He drove past Hamilton Development's Virginia office and decided to go home instead. It had been a long day and an even longer week. He needed to relax with a nice hot shower and a comfortable bed.

Chapter 11

The dreams came in an endless parade of erotic fantasies one right after the other, each more arousing and steamy than the last. In the first dream, Jordan was back on the deck of the ferry. Sheri was there in the darkness waiting for him when he walked out. He couldn't see her, but knew she was there. He sensed her. And then he felt her. She touched him. Her hand seemed to pass right through him. Almost immediately their clothes vanished. He reached out to her and felt the softness of her naked body.

He pressed her closer to him and they immediately connected. In an instant they were in each other's arms. He lifted her. She wrapped her legs around his body and there on the ferry deck, against the rail, they began to make sweet, precious love. It was a slow, seductive pleasure. In and out he dipped with every stroke, taking his time with each long, torturous withdrawal, then alternating with deep, penetrating thrusts. His eyelids were shut tightly as the seductive images faded in and out of his mind.

In his dream, they were outside on the beach under the stars. He lay back, still inside of her as she sat astride him, impaled atop his body. He felt her warmth and tightness surround him. He reached up and touched her face then let his hand gently roam down to her neck and shoulders. He cupped her breasts and ran his thumbs over her taut nipples. She gasped and arched her back. He leaned upward, captured and tasted the sweet flavor of her skin, the rounded flesh of her breasts and the pebbled bud of her nipple.

She gasped then plunged down onto him again and again, riding him in slow motion like the gentle waves that crested against their bodies. He watched her hips gyrate and felt his own need surge as their pace quickened. The rhythm of her body matched the beating of his heart. Soon they were insatiable in their pursuit of pleasure. Her body hovered low over his. He took her breasts into his mouth, tormenting her with the tip of his tongue as his hands massaged her rear, pressing her closer, deeper and harder.

He closed his eyes as his body tensed, drawing strength as he came closer to his climax. In the next dream the setting had changed again. They were in the trailer. He plunged into her with reckless abandon, pinning her back against his drawing table, which was almost at a right angle. They were a frantic coupling of raging desire. He suckled, she nibbled. He kissed, she burned. He felt the pain of her nails gouging his shoulders, but it didn't matter. Grinding, pumping, surging, their bodies were joined as their passions were the verge of an explosive release. Harder and deeper he thrust, angling his body just enough with each plunge to stimulate her engorged clitoris.

She moaned and groaned in fevered delight as he watched her come. Her eyes blazed with passion and desire as she seemed to beg for more, in fact demanded more. He readily obliged, watching her come again and again. He gave relentlessly. Then with unabashed need, he filled her with everything inside of him. They screamed their pleasure as his body stiffened and exploded, just as her image vanished. He reached out for her, but there was nothing—just air.

He awoke tangled in his bedsheets, while the dreams still echoed in his mind. He lay awake the rest of the night listening to the rain hitting the skylights above his bed. He reached out across the bed to the emptiness beside him, knowing he was alone and wondering what she was doing right now.

Sheri lay back, took a deep breath and released it slowly. Her heart still trembled. The dream was a mix of erotic foreplay and unsatisfied lust. It came out of nowhere and took her by surprise. She closed her eyes and willed her body to relax, but still her thoughts wandered back to her somnolent fantasy.

That's when she smelled it. It was a light woodsy scent. It was warm and comforting and it surrounded her. It seemed to reach out and touch her. She remembered it. Jordan wore that scent. She opened her eyes quickly, sat up and looked around. There was no one there, of course. But it seemed so real, felt so real, like he was actually there in the room with her.

She lay back down and closed her eyes again, this time letting the feeling overtake her. The scent was back and there was more. She felt his arm around her waist pulling her to his body just like before. This time she went willingly. The warmth of his breath caressed the nape of her neck. A superheated fluid that felt like molten lava flowed through her body. Then she felt his mouth on her neck—kissing her, teasing her and tasting her everywhere. She felt her body begin to warm.

She eased back as her body relaxed in what

seemed like slow motion. He was there with her. Their bodies merged and they began to move in a slow, undulating motion. Her thighs tensed as Jordan's desire began to seep inside her. She screamed his name over and over again as his sexual pleasure drove her beyond the brink of ecstasy.

She awoke moments later still calling his name. She opened her eyes and looked around. She realized she was alone in her bed in the middle of the night, her erotic dream interrupted by the rumble of thunder in the distance. She got up slowly and went to the balcony of her apartment. She opened the door and stepped outside.

The cool breeze immediately swept through her. There had been another brief rain shower and the temperature had dropped considerably. She wrapped her hands around her body and looked out across the courtyard. The quiet surroundings always gave her a sense of peace. Being on the top floor, she had the perfect view of downtown Crescent. Even with the heavy cloud cover and the cold, misty rain, she found the panoramic view comforting.

She tried to imagine what it was like almost a hundred and fifty years ago. Newly freed slaves were arriving on the island, hoping for a new life, a better life. They left a legacy of perseverance and determination—not just to survive but thrive—behind, providing historians a glimpse into their daily lives. She thought about Crescent Point. She had to do something. Future generations were depending on her to preserve that legacy.

What she didn't want to do was think about the dream she'd just had. But ignoring it wasn't working. Jordan was still on her mind. She licked her lips and almost tasted him. This was what her grandmother called her sensory gift. It was when she had a feeling inside that was so strong it took her to another place. She could sense what was about to happen. She could sense the future. But Sheri didn't want this future. As far as she was concerned, she and Jordan were never going to be together.

She turned abruptly and went back inside, closing and locking the balcony doors securely as if to close off her feelings. She lay back on the bed and willed herself to dream about something else, anything else. She drifted back to sleep, but couldn't shake his presence. So she gave in and dreamed about Jordan all over again.

Chapter 12

At about six o'clock, dawn finally pierced the Northern Virginia darkness. The day promised to be breezy, warm and partly sunny after a passing early-morning shower, according to the weatherman. Jordan was doubtful, however, despite the forecast. Lately, everything seemed to be conspiring against him.

It was still dark when he hit the road at half past six. He dipped his head low as the rain poured from the visor of his cap like a waterfall. The shower was more than he'd expected. But it didn't bother him. He barely noticed. Breathe in, breathe out. The four-mile jog he'd intended to make that morning had turned into a ten-mile run at marathon-speed. He needed this. Unfortunately, the harder he pushed the less he felt it. What was he thinking asking a question like that? No wonder he'd had erotic dreams last night.

He never gave in to emotion. It was a weakness he couldn't afford. And women were usually the cause of men becoming weak. His father had had a weakness for his mother until the day she walked out on him. Even after she left, he wanted her back. Jordan never could understand that. If that was love, he didn't want any part of it. He'd always told himself that it was against his nature to fall in love, and this was no time to start thinking otherwise.

He pressed harder still, running, working his body until he felt his legs begin to burn. A sleepless night could do that to a man. A troubled night could do that, too. But a restless, sleepless night thinking about Sheri Summers had done him in. Never had he experienced such a night of lustful torment before.

He ran across the open field, taking the long way back to his house. Set high in the hills of Northern Virginia, his home—which was originally an old farmhouse—was on an expansive four-acre lot with a creek and a pond. He'd bought the property and was taking his time restoring it. There was the main house, which he'd almost finished renovating—and a barn that he hoped to turn into his office and studio. It was a lengthy process, but one that he enjoyed immensely.

He ran along the outer perimeter of his property. A few years ago he'd paved a wide running path with motion detectors that turned on and off as he approached. From afar, it looked like a ring of lights rotating in a clockwise or counterclockwise sequence depending on which direction he ran. Since he loved to run outdoors and never had time, this was the perfect solution.

He made his last pass around the back lawn and headed toward the rear of the house. He slowed his pace as he approached, stretched and then climbed the stairs and went inside. He was exhausted, but he felt invigorated. His thoughts were clear and his mind was focused again. He headed up the back stairs to his large bedroom, peeled off his clothing then stepped into a hot shower. The steamy water pounded his body in a pulsating rhythm. It instantly reminded him of one of his dreams. He switched to cold water. A few minutes later he was feeling like his old self again. Afterward he shaved, dressed and headed into the office.

Jordan breezed into the headquarters of Hamilton Development as he had done a thousand times before. He was feeling good. Suddenly he felt a renewed sense of confidence that he knew exactly what he was going to do. He'd end their stalemate and get Sheri off his mind in the next few days.

He walked up the steps to the executive office level and as soon as he entered the main floor he could tell something was up. Wilamina Parker was sitting at the receptionist desk. As office manager she was in charge of nearly everything pertaining to the daily operations of the company. She was always meticulously organized and had impeccable judgment. She routinely hired and fired office staff, and apparently she'd gotten rid of another receptionist. She was on the phone and looked up as Jordan walked in.

Good morning, Jordan mouthed.

She ended her phone call and smiled happily. "Good morning, Jordan. How are you?"

"Fine, how's everything here?"

"Thankfully no drama so far, but as you know the day is just starting. But then again it's Friday, it's usually quiet by the end of the week." Just then her intercom feature beeped and one of the on-site managers spoke.

"Wilamina, we have a problem," the disembodied voice declared. She looked at Jordan and shook her head as she picked up the phone. "I guess I spoke too soon."

Jordan smiled and shook his head as he headed to his office. Once inside he dropped his briefcase and rolled the architectural plans out onto his desk then headed to the main conference room down the hall. His brothers sat around the table, waiting, while the company attorney, Kenneth, stood at the window talking on his cell phone.

Julian and Darius looked up as soon as Jordan walked in. Kenneth turned around, nodded and wrapped up the conversation. Both brothers looked at their watches. "It's about time," Julian said. "You're late. Our meetings start at seven o'clock."

"Of course he was late," Darius chuckled knowingly. "He was busy, weren't you, little brother?" They both laughed. It was obvious there was something he didn't know. He glanced over at Kenneth, who just shook his head. All three had grins on their faces as if they'd burst into laughter in the next second.

"What?" Jordan said, looking from one brother to another. Darius looked innocent. Julian chuckled and Kenneth looked away. "Okay, I get it. You know something I don't. Are you gonna tell me what it is or what?"

"I think we should let our little brother in on the joke."

Julian picked up a remote control, aimed it at the laptop computer on the conference room table and pressed a button. Jordan turned and waited. As soon as the picture came on he reached for the remote. Julian tossed it to Darius across the table. He caught it easily. Jordan just shook his head and waited to see the inevitable. It was exactly what he'd expected. It was the video of him and Sheri arguing, and him saving her from the backhoe. The look of passion in their eyes when they turned around was unmistakable. For the second time in less than a week Jordan's perfectly ordered life had been upended.

Sheri headed to work no closer to a solution to her problem than the night before. And now the problem had gotten even worse, of course. The fact that she and Jordan had been intimate definitely added to her dilemma. In just four days she'd lost her focus and couldn't stop thinking about him.

She'd been on edge all morning. Every time the phone rang she jumped, thinking it might be Jordan calling. She waited anxiously, but there was no word from him. She wasn't sure if she was relieved or not. Of course, she didn't tell anyone about what had happened between them. After all, it was a mistake, twice. But avoiding him wasn't going to solve her problem. By midmorning she gave in and called Hamilton Development. Tamika answered and told her that Jordan was out of the office. She didn't leave a message.

She tried to avoid thinking about him the rest of the morning, but the image of their affair crept into her thoughts at the most inopportune moments. She was on a conference call with another museum making arrangements for an exhibit transfer and noted the curator had the same last name. She even asked if they might be related. It was crazy. It was insane. What in the world was she doing and what did she expect to happen—for him to be thinking about her, too? Clearly he had to have at least a dozen women who were after him.

The thing is, if he hadn't gotten her so upset she never would have kissed him in the first place, and things wouldn't have gotten out of hand. It was unprofessional and totally out of character for her. But deep down inside she enjoyed it. Just thinking about it made her insides quiver even now.

She could see why women probably swooned when he walked by. He practically swept her off her feet. Heaven knows the man was an incredible lover. He was insatiable. They both had given as much as they took. There was no asking or wondering about the sexual ground rules. She just did whatever her body dictated and she liked it. She liked it too much.

Now all she kept thinking about was what happened in Jordan's trailer. She imagined them on his drafting table, in his private quarters; the memories were vivid and sensuous. It was fantasy, but it was also much more. It seemed as if all of her senses were attuned to him. His scent, his taste, his touch was in perfect harmony with her body. They made love in every position and every place imaginable. "Good Lord," she muttered to herself, feeling a sudden surge of heat course through her body.

"Huh, what?" Genie said.

Sheri looked up. Her mind had wandered again. She was in her office and Genie was across the room.

"Did you say something to me?" Genie asked.

"No, nothing," Sheri muttered.

"Oh, okay. Well, as I was saying, Jamie just texted me again. I guess whatever you said to Mr. Hamilton the last time must have worked. No one's been up at the site since we left. At least that's good news, right?" she said.

Sheri nodded. "Did your boyfriend mention if Jordan was at work today?"

"No, he just said they've stopped working on the site for the time being. He tried to go up there, but one of the guards told him he couldn't." She started texting again then a few minutes later replied. "He said he thinks Jordan Hamilton left the island last night."

"He left last night?" Sheri repeated.

"Yeah, Jamie just texted that he doesn't work on Fridays and Mondays," she added. "It must be nice."

"Yeah, I guess so," Sheri said in a distracted voice, realizing that Jordan had probably been on his way off the island when she went over there yesterday.

"Okay." Genie stood and brought the books back over to Sheri's desk. "I looked up everything you wanted me to. I gotta get back down to the gift shop. My shift begins in five minutes. Let me know if you hear anything. Don't forget you have a program scheduled for middle-school students this afternoon."

"I won't," Sheri said. "See you later." As soon as Genie left, Sheri turned back to her computer. She was relieved, but her mind was still far away. At least he was off the island until Monday, she thought. She didn't have to worry about him stopping by the museum or bumping into him someplace else.

Thankfully it was Friday, which was almost always her busiest day, and today there were two groups of students coming in. She enjoyed talking to the kids and getting them interested in local history. She also had several back-to-back meetings scheduled in the morning and she planned to be out of the museum that afternoon. Keeping busy was the perfect distraction.

Sheri decided to go to see her former stepfather again and ask if he could come up with a solution to her dispute with Jordan Hamilton. After all, he was head of the city council. Surely there was something he could do. It was the council that had approved Hamilton to develop the resort on the land in the first place. She knew the historical significance of the site probably wouldn't sway him. If it was about making money he was all too happy to go along.

After her meeting with Nolan Chambers she headed back to the museum. She waved to the museum security guards as she entered. As she always did, she glanced up at the museum's signage. A feeling of pride and satisfaction suffused her every time she entered the museum. The building was old and in need of repair, and at times it seemed to be crumbling down around them. But it was a monument to those who founded Crescent Island.

There were two floors of exhibition space and an archival storage area that was almost a century old. The main wing was dedicated to *Mabella Louisa* and was sponsored by the Gates Heritage Foundation. Two of the smaller exhibits were being returned. She was working on the transfer now. She had immersed herself in work until she was interrupted by her cell phone ringing. She picked it up without looking at the caller ID.

"Sheri Summers."

"Hi. I hear you called looking for me."

She stopped working and tried to swallow the lump in her throat. She knew exactly who it was. She hadn't left a message and there was no way

Tamika, his office assistant, could have known it was her. Still… She paused briefly. "Hi. Thanks for returning my call."

"I would have called sooner had you left a message."

"I hope I'm not disturbing you."

"No, not at all, Sheri. How are you?"

"Good, and you?"

"Much better now, what can I do for you?"

"I think perhaps we should talk and I mean really talk. I'd like to meet with you this afternoon and discuss this situation."

"I'm afraid that won't be possible."

"I understand you're busy, but…"

"Yes, I am busy. But I'm also no longer on the island," Jordan explained.

"Oh, I see," she said softly. "Well, is there someone else I can speak to about this matter?"

"Sheri, like I said last night, I understand your position. Please understand mine. I cannot and will not shut down my construction site for you or anyone else."

She paused a moment. "I see. Thank you for your time. Goodbye." She hung up. A moment later her cell phone rang again. She looked at the caller ID. It was Jordan. "Hello."

"Meet me tonight," he said.

"I can't. I'm going to a party this evening."

"At Gates Manor?" he guessed.

"Yes."

"Good. I'll meet you there."

Sheri hung up the phone and stared at it. "What just happened?" she said.

Genie stopped at the open door to Sheri's office. "Are you still here? Don't you have a meeting in town?"

Sheri glanced at her watch. She was already five minutes late. "I gotta go." She grabbed her bag and headed out.

The day had turned out to be a slow-paced Friday instead. After the morning meeting with his brothers and Kenneth and the little sideshow they pulled, Jordan spent the rest of the morning signing off on paperwork and sat at his desk researching his next project. He called and talked to Tamika and Ian about the break-in he and Cleveland had discussed the night before. The return call from Tamika was unexpected. Her message was even more unexpected.

When he hung up from Tamika he called Sheri. An hour later he was headed back to Crescent Island. Initially, he'd had no intention of going back until next week. And there was no way he had expected to attend the event at Gates Manor tonight. But today was different.

He got to the work site around four o'clock. He stayed in the trailer taking care of details he could

have handled from the main office or that could
have waited until next week.

In truth, he didn't want to admit why he actually came back to the island. As soon as he walked
into the trailer he saw the business card he left on
the desk the day before. He picked it up and sat
down. She was the reason he returned. There was
something about her that made him want to know
more. And one night with her was never going to
be enough. He turned on his laptop and looked up
the Crescent Island Museum. He expected the site
to be pretty standard and uninteresting. Instead,
what he found was an informative site dedicated
to what looked like a remarkable institution.

Later, after a restless hour or so, he stood,
stretched and walked over to the trailer window.
It was much later than he thought. It was already
getting dark and most of the workers had already
left for the day. A few stragglers headed toward the
gate and Cleveland and his crew walked around
patrolling the site. Just as he went back to his desk
and sat down, Ian came in. He was carrying a large
box. "Hey," he said, surprised. "I didn't know you
were here. "When did you get in?"

Jordan looked at his watch. "A couple of hours
ago," he said.

"It's Friday, you never come on-site Fridays and
Mondays. What's going on, everything okay?"

"Yeah, just tying up a few loose ends. Is there anything happening here?"

Ian frowned. "Just the usual. Why?"

"I wondered if the museum called or sent someone over."

"No, not that I know of. Were you expecting someone?"

"No, probably not," he said. Ian started chuckling. Jordan turned to him. "What?"

"So, what's the deal with the two of you?" Ian asked.

"The two of who?" Jordan responded.

Ian chuckled. "You and the museum lady," he clarified.

"I don't know what you're talking about."

"Yeah, okay," Ian said slyly.

"So what's in the box?" Jordan asked, changing the subject.

"Leroy said you wanted anything that came out of that hole up on the mound. It took him a while to sort it out. Apparently one of the new guys decided he wanted a bunch of keepsakes. I think some of the stuff he had was headed to eBay. The larger pieces, mainly wood planks, are in the holding shed out back."

Jordan got up and walked over to the side table and looked inside the box. There were several small shards of wood, an old medicine bottle and a few smaller items that looked like trash. "Has anyone been up there since we talked?"

"Just Cleveland. He set the camera up earlier."

"Good." He picked up each piece and examined it then placed it on his desk. Afterward he shook his head. "It all looks like trash to me."

"Yeah, me, too. But what do I know?"

Jordan put the pieces back in the box then picked up the bottle to examine it more closely. "There's something written on this and a date on the bottle, but I can't quite make it out. And what's this—it looks like an oversize golf tee, but it's hollow."

Ian walked over to the desk. "You know I used to play the trumpet years and years ago. This looks like a mouthpiece for a horn."

"Yeah, you're right, it does." He picked up the bottle again and looked at it more closely. "I think I'll head into town this weekend and stop by one of the antique shops. Perhaps they can give me some more information."

"Good idea. Are you leaving now?" Ian asked.

"In a little bit."

"Are you heading back home for the weekend?"

"Actually, I have a party to attend this evening here on the island," Jordan said, gathering his things and the box on the side table. "And a very interesting woman to meet."

"Sounds good," Ian said. "Enjoy."

Jordan smiled as soon as the door closed.

Chapter 13

By the time Sheri got back to the museum she was completely frazzled. She'd done her job; she'd entertained the kids while teaching them a little bit of history. She talked about the museum, the island's history and some of the digs she'd been on. They loved it. But the entire time her mind was a hundred miles away. "No, stop thinking about it," she said aloud. "It was just a momentary lapse in judgment. It didn't mean anything." She quickly pulled around to the rear of the building, parked and got out. She hurried up the front steps just as the museum was about ready to close for the day. She walked into the main lobby and past the last few patrons still walking around looking at the exhibits. She was headed to her office when she heard her name.

She turned and realized that she'd just walked right by her friends Madison Gates and Kennedy Mason. They walked up behind her. She stopped and covered her mouth realizing she'd completely forgotten she was supposed to meet them for a late lunch. She hurried over to them with open arms. "Oh, no, Madi, Keni, I'm so sorry. I completely forgot about meeting you guys today. Have you been here the whole time?"

"No, we went shopping and just got back," Madison said.

"Girl, you are in so much trouble," Kennedy joked. "You'd better have a good excuse for standing us up."

"Oh, you would not believe the week I've been having. From the moment I walked in Monday morning, things have been crazy. Come on. Let's get you signed in and then go up to my office. We can talk there."

"Isn't the museum about to close?"

Sheri looked at her watch. It was a few minutes after four o'clock. "Don't worry, it's okay, come on." She took them to the security station and waited as they showed ID and signed in. Afterward, they headed up the stairs, then to her office. "It's so good to see you guys. So wait, where are the kids?"

"They're at the house with Mamma Lou, Camille and the nannies. They insisted on babysitting today so we could hang out."

"I can't wait to see them. How old are the twins now?" she asked Madison.

"They're almost three years old," Madison said.

"Already, I can't believe it. Time flies. And Kennedy what about Nya, how old is she now?" she asked, turning to Kennedy.

"Nya's almost five months. She laughs and smiles and babbles all the time. She tries to grab everything she sees—earrings, necklaces, glasses. She loves cell phones just like the twins."

Sheri smiled and giggled. "Aw, that's so sweet. I can't wait to see them. So when did you get here?"

"Tony, Madison and I got here this afternoon around one o'clock," Kennedy said. Madison nodded her confirmation. "Juwan is coming later this evening. He's in D.C. right now."

"It feels so good to be back on the island again," Madison said. "It's been forever. I really missed being here. I know it's part of Virginia, but it always feels so remote."

They got to Sheri's office. She unlocked the door and they went inside. She forgot she had left her desk a mess. It looked like a tornado had touched down. There were papers, charts, maps and open books everywhere. She immediately walked over to her desk and began organizing the books and storing away the maps and charts. Since both Madison and Kennedy worked in the arts, she knew they wouldn't be too surprised to see her office in such a mess. Madison was an art history professor in Philadelphia and Kennedy worked as a museum curator in Washington, D.C. "Have a seat. Sorry, the place is such a mess. I ran out of here like the devil was hot on my tail."

"Yeah, that's what one of the employees downstairs said earlier. So, what happened? You looked completely stressed out rushing in here just now. Is everything okay?"

Sheri sat down and shook her head. "No, not really. This week has just been crazy. I have no idea what I'm doing anymore."

"What do you mean? What happened?"

Sheri shook her head. "I got turned down for the permanent position as curator here."

"What?" Kennedy and Madison said.

"I was told I didn't have the passion for it."

"That's crazy."

"Then Genie, my assistant, got a text message about some artifacts found on a construction site. I don't know if you know this story, but this island was originally named after a freed slave ship that left port in Maryland intent on sailing back to Africa."

"Yes, the *Crescent*," Madison said. Kennedy nodded.

"That's right," Sheri said. "Well, it looks like there's a very real possibility that the wreckage from the *Crescent* may have been found."

"Oh, that's wonderful. That's amazing," both sisters said at the same time.

"Have you started excavations?" Madison asked excitedly. "We'd love to see it while we're here on the island. It must be awesome."

"Oh, yeah, definitely," Kennedy added. "We gotta see it."

"I wish we could, but we can't," Sheri said.

"Why not?" Madison asked. "Is the site closed?"

"Something like that. It's out on Crescent Point, right by the inlet. There's construction going on in the area. They're building a resort," she said drily. "Right over it."

Both Madison and Kennedy picked up on her tone. "What? They can't do that," Kennedy said. "It's a historical site."

"They can and they are. The company bought the property. Apparently they can do whatever they want with it. The main structure is almost complete. The artifacts were actually found at a secondary location."

"What did the Smithsonian say?"

"They're looking into it, but it's obvious my boss isn't taking this seriously. The developer is a major contributor to the Smithsonian."

"Do you know for sure what's out there?"

"That's just it, I don't. I saw pieces of wood resembling the hull of a ship. It's promising. When this construction company cleared the debris and dug a hole, it flooded the site. They drained it. That's where I was earlier this week. I was trying to convince the owner to close the site for a few days or at the very least allow me to take samples, so I could have them examined and carbon tested."

"I gather he said no."

"Of course he did. He's one of those don't-stand-in-the-way-of-progress people. He'd steamroll the pyramids to make way for a parking lot and shopping mall if given half a chance. I'm sorry. I know I sound callous. When I think about it I get so angry. How can he not see the importance of finding out for sure? If I'm wrong, then so be it. But if I'm right and what's on his property is the actually the wreckage of the *Crescent* then it changes everything. History gets rewritten. It means the *Crescent* never made it back to Africa, which refutes what historians have long believed."

Madison and Kennedy could see and understand her passion. They nodded. "Okay, so what can we do to help?"

"I'm going to try and convince him to see what he's sacrificing. If that doesn't work I'm going to my uncle's office. He's a judge. I'll ask him to grant me an immediate injunction."

"Can he do that without sufficient proof?"

"I have proof, sort of. It's probably tenuous at best. I've pulled maps and charts and a ledger that was found a century ago. There's a possibility it could put the *Crescent* in that exact location if it were shipwrecked."

"Will you have enough time? How long do you think an emergency injunction would last?" Madison asked.

"Seventy-two hours, that's not a lot of time," Kennedy said, having had experience with injunctions before.

"I'm hoping I can gather samples and at least get the process started. If time runs out I'm hoping I can get a court order."

"You know his lawyers are going to be all over this," Madison said. "Can't you talk to him, maybe explain the historical significance of this find?"

Sheri shook her head. "I tried. He's adamant. He won't listen."

"Maybe he just needs the right persuasion," Madison said. Kennedy nodded her agreement.

"Like what?"

"Show him Crescent Island. Let him see and experience the history and magnificence of what the locals call God's garden."

Sheri took a deep breath and released it slowly while shaking her head. "I have to tell you there's more to all of this. We've met before."

"When?" Madison asked.

"About nine months ago, Mamma Lou introduced us." Madison and Kennedy looked at each other. "She was playing matchmaking."

"I assume it didn't exactly work out."

Sheri shook her head. "Not even close. I think we purposely turned away from each other just because Mamma Lou tried to put us together."

"So what's he like?"

"He's a typical know-it-all, egocentric, condescending, pain in the neck."

Madison and Kennedy laughed. "Now what's he really like?"

"He's intelligent, attractive, sexy, funny and very talented. He's an architect and his work is brilliant."

"Sounds like you might kinda like him," Kennedy said.

"Yes, I'm attracted to him," Sheri admitted.

"Is that all?" Madison asked. Sheri didn't respond.

"Truthfully, I don't know what to think. He drives me crazy and sometimes all I can think about is seeing him."

"That sounds very familiar," Madison said smiling. Kennedy nodded.

"What do you mean?" Sheri asked.

"It was the same way with me and Tony when we first met. The man drove me insane. Everything about him was wrong for me. He was all those things and more. After a while I saw beyond all that other stuff. I have a feeling your guy is the same way. Maybe you should look beyond what you see."

"Same with me, when I first met Juwan we argued constantly. There was no way we were ever going to get along. Then all of a sudden I saw his heart and his spirit. I fell in love without even knowing it was happening. I believed I was saving him from deportation. What I got instead is a fairy-tale life as a real princess. My life has never been the same."

"Yeah, but that's you guys. You both met incredible men and now live incredible lives. It was a once or rather twice in a lifetime thing. That'll never happen to me and certain not with Jordan."

"You never know."

"When we kissed…"

"Wait, you kissed?" Kennedy asked. Kennedy and Madison looked at each other then back at Sheri. Sheri looked mortified.

"Not just that. Last night I went to the construction site to talk and one thing led to another and we made love. I know, I know. It's crazy. It's wrong, it's unprofessional and I still don't know what happened. One minute we were arguing and the next thing I knew we were in each other's arms kissing like we were long-lost lovers. He had a bedroom in his trailer and we made love. I swear my toes curled, my knees buckled, my stomach felt like I'd swallowed a jackhammer and every nerve ending in my body liquefied like hot lava." She shivered.

"Wow, that sounds like some kind of incredible evening."

"Believe me, it was. The man is talented and I'm not just talking about as an architect." She looked at Madison and Kennedy, knowing they knew exactly what she was talking about. Sheri sighed, shaking her head and licking her lips. "Now I don't know what to do. I've lost all credibility in this."

"Maybe not," Kennedy said hopefully.

"Yes," Madison added quickly, "maybe not."

"Yes, I have, I know it. After we made love do you really think he's going to listen to me or take me seriously?"

"Make him listen."

"Yes, find him, take him out and show him the Crescent Island you know and love. Show him your passion. Maybe he'll see it, too."

"He wants to meet tonight at the party."

Madison looked at her watch. "Oh, speaking of tonight, we'd better get going. It's getting late," Madison said as she and Kennedy stood to leave. Sheri came around to the front of her desk. "We'll see you tonight, right?"

"Yes, I'll be there. But I'm not staying long. My grandmother and Mamma Lou are still on a match-making mission and you know what that means," Sheri said.

"Definitely," Kennedy said, and then hugged Sheri warmly.

"Are you leaving now?" Madison asked, hugging her next.

"No. I have a few more things to take care of here. But I'll see you guys tonight."

"Okay."

Madison and Kennedy left Sheri's office and took the stairs down to the main level. The museum was closed and completely empty except for the security guards still at their station. Madison and Kennedy signed out and left. While heading to the car, Madison smiled happily. "How does she do it?"

"Mamma Lou? I have no idea," Kennedy said.

"She introduced them months ago. They dismissed each other and now they can't keep their hands off each other. It's like some kind of matchmaking ESP."

Kennedy shook her head. "Yeah I know, she's right in the center of Mamma Lou's bull's-eye and doesn't even know it. Think we should warn her?" Kennedy asked.

"No way, let's wait and see. You never know, love comes to people in the most peculiar ways," Madison said.

"Okay, now you're scaring me. You're starting to sound just like Mamma Lou."

They laughed as they got into the car. "Sheri

didn't mention his name, who do you think it is?" Madison asked.

Kennedy shrugged. "I don't know, but I have feeling we're gonna find out real soon."

Madison smiled and nodded. "Me, too. It's the perfect day to observe romance in the making, isn't it?"

Kennedy looked at her sister shaking her head. "Careful or we're gonna have to start calling you Mamma Madi."

Chapter 14

Camille Rantone and Louise Gates sat outside under the covered patio with the fireplace blazing on Friday evening. Earlier that day they had watched the sun dip below the horizon, and now patiently waited for the guests to arrive. There was a warm luminous glow surrounding them as they talked quietly and anticipated enjoying the approaching evening. "Thank you, Louise, it's the perfect evening to have this celebration," Camille said.

Louise nodded. "It's my pleasure, Cam, and you're right, this is a gorgeous night. It's hard to believe it's already fall. Where does the time go?"

Camille sighed as her eyes watered. "I've been

asking myself that a lot lately. I see so much. But I didn't see our enduring friendship. Do you know we met more than sixty years ago? Since then our journeys have taken so many twists and turns along the path to love and happiness. Life, death, joy and sorrow, our friendship has lasted through it all. You were there when my world fell apart so many times—the deaths of two wonderful husbands."

Louise reached out and took Camille's hand. "And you were there for me. We're family, Cam, sisters of the heart. Ever since the evening we met in that tent when Emma begged me to go in and see you."

"I miss her," Camille said softly.

"Yes, me, too. So very much," Louise muttered quietly. "Her life and her work are a testament to the woman she was. She achieved everything you told her she would. Thank you for that."

"Oh, my, how in the world did we get to such a sad place?" Camille asked. "Tonight is supposed to be a celebration of life and history."

"We're old, we're allowed. So have you spoken with Sheri?"

"Earlier, she's coming."

"Good," Louise said.

Camille sighed. "To tell you the truth, Louise, I'm not sure what to do anymore," Camille said. "Sheri is just so much like her mother, stubborn and pigheaded. And she keeps her head in those books.

How is she ever going to find someone if she never leaves the museum?"

"Give her time, Camille. She'll come around."

Camille shook her head again. "But will it be too late? I wish I could see her future like I can see everyone else's. I see strangers with perfect clarity."

"Your gift doesn't work like that and you know it. You can see everyone's future except those closest to you. It's your love and emotional attachment that blocks you. It blinds you to the truth, the future, in your loved ones. Sheri's your granddaughter. You've never been able to read her before and you never will."

"I know. That's why I need you to do this for me. Find her match. Find a man who will appreciate her passion."

Louise glanced around slowly to make sure that Colonel Wheeler was inside. She was free to talk openly. "I promised Otis I wouldn't do any more matchmaking until I picked a date for our wedding, but I think this would be considered an emergency and just one last time would be okay. After all, she is family."

Camille reached over and held Louise's hand. "Now you know I can't see your future anymore. But I do know your wedding will be a spectacular event right here at this house. There's also a feeling of warmth surrounding you. That much I do see."

Louise nodded. "That was just the confirmation

I needed. I was thinking the exact same thing, getting married right here at the manor. The family together where it all began, it's the perfect location."

"I agree. It's so lovely here, particularly in spring," Camille said.

"Yes, a spring wedding would be ideal. The weather would be perfect, not too cold and not too warm. Yes. That's it." She nodded decisively. "Now let's get back to the business at hand—Sheri," Louise said quietly as she leaned closer. "I believe I have the perfect man in mind for her. I invited him tonight, but I'm not sure if he'll come. He's about as stubborn and determined as Sheri is. I introduced them a few months ago, but they fought so hard against the attraction nothing came of it. There was definitely a spark. Now I believe the timing is just right again. They're that perfect match of opposites attract. They'll do very well together. "

"If they give love a chance," Camille said wistfully.

"Yes, but I'm hopeful they will, perhaps even tonight. Then if we're lucky, we'll get a chance to see the spark ignite once more."

Camille sighed. "I'm almost ninety years old. Time isn't exactly on my side these days. I'd love to see her happily married soon."

"Don't worry, Cam. I'm already on the job."

"On what job?" The question suddenly coming from behind them surprised the two. They turned and looked up. Colonel Otis Wheeler stood with his arms crossed "What are you two ladies up to?" he queried, knowing the answer to his question. When Camille and Louise put their heads together things happened.

The women did their best to look innocent, but failed miserably. "What on earth makes you think we're up to something?" Louise said. "We're just sitting here enjoying the evening and having a great conversation about spring weather."

Colonel Wheeler chuckled. "Uh-huh, right," he said, not buying a word of it. "Now I may not be able to see the future and I don't have the gift of matchmaking, but I do know a couple of scheming ladies when I see them."

Camille laughed heartily as Louise pretended to be insulted.

"Well, now, how do you like that," Louise said. "So much for love and trust." Then she turned to Camille, who was still laughing. "Now, don't you go encouraging him."

"My darling," Colonel Wheeler said, taking Louise's hand tenderly. "I do trust you and you know I love you. I also know when you're up to something. And you, my dear, are always up to something. Matchmaking, I'd surmise."

Still pretending to be innocent, Louise opened her mouth in shock. Camille laughed harder. Unable to keep a straight face, Louise finally joined in the laughter. "I think I just got my answer," Colonel Wheeler said.

"Hey, sounds like there's a party going on out here."

Camille, Louise and Otis turned around to see Tony and Madison walking out onto the patio with their twins, Johanna and Jonathan, running behind them. "Look who's here," Louise said, opening her arms for the twins to come to her. They ran and were immediately swallowed up with hugs, kisses and love. Everyone started talking all at once. It was the beginning of a joyous celebration. A few minutes later Randolph and Juliet walked in along with Kennedy, Juwan and their newborn daughter, Nya. A number of guests arrived soon after. Family, old friends, new friends and somewhere along the way Louise and Camille realized this was all the time they needed.

Chapter 15

For years Sheri grew up going to Gates Manor thinking it was no big deal. Her mother and grandmother would bring her along, and Louise Gates became like another grandparent to her. Louise's grandsons, Antonio and Raymond, were like her big brothers. As kids they teased and drove her crazy. In turn she'd follow them everywhere. They'd all hang out together and she tried her best to tag along. As they grew older, their paths took different directions, but they still stayed close. It wasn't until she was in high school that she realized how special a gift it was to be part of the Gates family.

In her college years, they grew even closer and seemed to always be around one another. They visited each other in college and traveled together during breaks. All of her college friends had crushes on Sheri's brothers, Daniel and Mark, as well Tony and Ray. Everyone knew the Gates family on Crescent Island and she was part of the family.

Going to a party at Gates Manor was in some people's minds akin to attending a state dinner at the White House. Few were invited and if you were blessed enough to be included, it was definitely a good idea to go. Louise Gates was the unofficial first lady of Crescent Island. Everyone knew her and adored her.

As usual, the stately old house looked spectacular. Built in the 1960s, it was impressive from every angle. The front porch was completely illuminated when every light in the house was on. It was stunning. She hurried along the redbrick driveway then walked up the steps to the wraparound porch, hoping to have a nice relaxing evening with her family and friends as long as she could steer clear of Mamma Lou and her matchmaking.

As she opened the door and walked in, a sense of joy and happiness hit her. It was good to be surrounded by family and friends.

"Sheri, there you are. You look beautiful," her mother said, crossing the room to meet her. She linked arms with her daughter and tilted her head to the side. "I have the perfect man for you."

"Oh, Mom, please, not you, too."

"I'm afraid so. But trust me on this one, he's perfect. Now where did he go? Ah, there he is talking to Tony. Come on, I'll point you in the right direction. Go introduce yourself. He's in the family room."

"Okay, I will, but first I want to see Grandma and Mamma Lou."

Following his GPS directions, Jordan arrived at the entrance to the manor in less time than he'd expected. He stopped and looked up at the iron gates then down the illuminated driveway to see the stately home perched on a small hill. "Now this is what I call a driveway," he said aloud. The car behind him flashed its lights. He glanced in the rearview mirror, waved then drove up the extended driveway and rounded the circular path in front of Gates Manor.

He drove back down near to the end of the driveway, parked and got out. He looked up, admiring the home as he approached. A white colonial mansion, it was nothing short of magnificent. Stately and dignified, it reminded him a lot of its owner, Louise Gates. The road was lined with what looked like century-old oak trees that stood like royal sentries along the path. It was all wonderfully dramatic.

The building itself was rectangular, with a wraparound porch connected to a covered portico with huge white columns. Jordan walked up the wooden steps to the porch and rang the doorbell. Seconds later the door was answered. An attractive middle-aged woman greeted him with a warm, welcoming smile. "Good evening, please, come in. Welcome to Gates Manor."

"Thank you, good evening," he said, walking into the foyer. "I'm a guest of Louise Gates."

"Then you had better call her Mamma Lou, hadn't you? Everyone else does."

"Yes, so I've been told, repeatedly." He looked around at the guests mingling, laughing and talking in the living room and in what looked like a solarium. Everyone seemed to be having a great time. "Wow, I didn't expect so many people. Mamma Lou mentioned it would be a small gathering. It looks like nearly everybody on the island showed up."

"When Louise Gates throws a party, it's a very big deal. If you're on the island it's a must to attend. And actually, to Louise, this *is* a small gathering. I'm Lois Chambers," the woman said, extending her hand and introducing herself. "And you are…"

"I'm Jordan Hamilton. Nice to meet you, Mrs. Chambers."

"Call me Lois, please. And it's a pleasure meeting you, as well. So Jordan, what do you do for a living?" she asked.

"I'm in construction," he said.

"Jordan Hamilton, you wouldn't happen to be one of the Hamilton brothers from Hamilton Development Corporation?"

"I am."

Lois smiled brightly. "Of course, my ex-husband has mentioned you often. You know him, of course, his name is Nolan Chambers. He's head of the city council. He speaks very highly of you. It's wonderful to finally meet you. I understand your resort complex is going to be sensational."

"I certainly hope so," he said, looking around.

"I'm looking forward to seeing it when it's completed."

"We're planning a big opening."

"So tell me, Jordan," she began as she glanced behind him, "will your wife or fiancée be joining you this evening?"

"No," he said, deciding not to give more information than asked.

"Then perhaps you and your girlfriend—" She probed further.

"No girlfriend, either," he interrupted then watched her smile that smile and knew it was time to change the subject. This wasn't the first time a woman tried to hook him up with their daughter, niece or granddaughter and it certainly wouldn't be the last. He'd been getting this special attention all his adult life, and more and more recently. The result was always disastrous. Jordan changed the subject. "This is a magnificent home."

"Yes, it is. I assume this your first time here?"

"Yes."

"Well, then, come in, I'll show you around," Lois said, linking her arm in his. They walked into the living room then continued through to the dining room, where they stopped and got a drink. Lois talked about the history of the home and gave a brief history of when Louise and her then-husband, Jonathan Gates, had it built. They continued into the enormous family and game room. There were a lot more people there than he'd expected. Lois introduced Jordan to some of the family and guests as they walked through. They stayed and talked with a small group that included Tony and Madison Gates and Kennedy Evans-Mason.

"So how did you meet Mamma Lou?" Madison asked Jordan.

"She played matchmaker with my older brother, Julian, and his wife, Dena. Dena's aunt is a friend of hers. Ellen Peyton."

All three smiled and nodded. "That sounds familiar," Tony said. "My grandmother's been matching up couples forever. My cousin and I have joked over the years that she should open her own matchmaking firm."

"That's probably a great idea. She'd make a mint," said Madison.

"Is she really that good at it?" Jordan asked.

"Yes," all three answered together then laughed.

"Let's see," Madison began, "there's you and me. Kennedy, you and Juwan."

"My father and uncles along with their wives. My cousin Raymond and his wife, Hope," Tony continued.

"JT and Juliet, her friend Patricia and Franklin, Randolph and Alyssa, Trey and Kenya," Kennedy added then paused.

"And also my brother Julian and Dena," Jordan said. "Wow, that's a lot of matchmaking."

"Yeah, tell me about it. And those are just the ones we know about. Imagine all the rest we don't know about."

"So what do you do, Jordan?" Kennedy asked.

"I'm an architect and developer. My company, Hamilton Development, is building a resort out on Crescent Point."

Madison nearly choked on her wine. She realized exactly who he was. Tony patted her back gently. "Are you okay, babe?" he said. She nodded and looked at Kennedy who was nearly bursting at the seams.

"Aha, Jordan, so you're the one, huh?" Kennedy said.

"The one?" Jordan wondered aloud, and quickly assumed that Kennedy didn't agree with all the development on the island.

"Yes, the one building at Crescent Point. I hear you are extremely talented," Kennedy said.

Madison choked again, knowing that Kennedy was using Sheri's words when she had described the kiss earlier. Tony patted her back again. "Are you sure you're okay?" Tony asked. She nodded again.

"We heard it's going to be stunning," Kennedy continued.

"It's going to be nice," he said modestly. "Unfortunately, I've gotten quite a bit of opposition."

"Change is difficult, particularly in a small place like Crescent Island. But I wouldn't worry. As soon as the project is complete everyone who opposed it will certainly come around when they see how much revenue it brings to the island."

Jordan nodded. "I hope so. Do you work on the island?"

"Yes, I own an antique shop. I have locations here, in Alexandria, in Philadelphia and now in New York," said Tony.

"Antiques, huh? That's exactly what I'm looking for. I'd like to stop by and show you a few things that have crossed my desk recently. Maybe you can point me in the right direction."

"Sure," Tony said. "I'll be in the store tomorrow. Why don't you stop by?"

"I will. Thanks."

The conversation continued, then switched to construction and then on to the beauty of Crescent Island. A number of guests joined their little group and for the next forty-five minutes Jordan smiled, shook hands and joked with Tony, Madison, Kennedy and other guests. He gave out business cards when asked, made business contacts to help expand the Hamilton Development name.

He blended in easily with the crowd. With the businessmen, he talked about what was happening in the market. With sports fans he talked about the upcoming seasons and with the politicians he spoke with conviction about the state of local and national issues. He was charming and always made a good impression. He'd been doing it his entire life.

Juwan Mason, Kennedy's husband, and doctors Raymond and Hope arrived just as Jordan had planned to leave. He stayed a bit longer hoping Sheri would still come. After a while he noticed the party was beginning to thin. It was time for him to make his move as the conversation turned back to Mamma Lou and her upcoming wedding to Colonel Wheeler.

"Where is Mamma Lou?" Jordan asked.

"I believe she's outside on the patio."

Jordan turned and looked out through the open French doors. He saw her instantly. His face lit up. He excused himself and made his way toward the patio, following Sheri.

"Good evening."

She turned around and smiled. "Hi, you made it."

"Yes, I did." He openly looked down the length of her body and raked his lower lip with his teeth. "You look stunning."

"Thank you. You look very handsome, too."

For a moment they didn't speak, just stood smiling at each other. "I guess one of us should say something. We can't just stand here staring at each other."

"Dance with me," he whispered.

There was soft jazz playing, but no one was dancing. Sheri looked around. "I don't know if you noticed or not, but no one's dancing."

"Don't worry. They'll join us in a few minutes."

She nodded. He took her hand and guided her outside onto the patio near the pool. There was crystal light in the trees and candles floating in the pool. They were surrounded by more open space. He wrapped his arm around her body and pulled her close. They began moving to the slow rhythms.

It took less than a few minutes before others joined them, as Jordan had predicted. Tony took

Madison's hand and brought her out onto the patio. The expressions on their faces was unmistakable. Seeing Tony, Juwan held out his hand to his wife, Kennedy. She took it and followed him as did JT and Juliet, her baby bump several months along by now. Raymond looked around the room for his wife. She was talking. He touched her hand. She turned. When he smiled and glanced toward the patio, she nodded and followed him. Soon more couples were dancing.

"You are a genius," Sheri whispered. "How did you know?"

"It only takes one."

Sheri nodded and leaned closer, enjoying the moment. She looked around at the happy couples and then up at the stars in the sky. "It's so beautiful tonight. It's the perfect moment. I wish…" she began then stopped herself.

He leaned back and looked at her. "What?" he asked.

She shook her head. "Nothing."

"No, tell me. What did you wish?"

"I wish this feeling would last forever."

He looked deep into her eyes. His heart poured out to her. She was beautiful, but not just her face or her body, even though they certainly were. It was her spirit he loved. "Me, too." He wrapped his arm tighter around her waist and held her close. A feeling of contentment filled him. He looked around at the many couples near them. They all had the same expression as his brother Julian. "Me, too," he whispered again.

After the next two songs ended Sheri took Jordan's hand. "Come, I want you to meet someone." They walked around to the covered patio area. There were a number of guests surrounding an older woman. She sat telling a most interesting tale about early Crescent Island history and folklore. Even though she appeared to be well into her eighties her voice was clear and strong. They only caught the ending of her story, but he found it fascinating.

When she ended, there was a collective sigh and jubilant applause. Several of the guests sitting around thanked her and then got up to leave. Others wandered back into the house.

"Hi, Grandma. Hi, Mamma Lou," Sheri said, bending down to kiss their cheeks. "That was a wonderful tale. I don't remember hearing it before."

"I still have a few secrets," Camille said, and winked. "Sheri, be a dear and get me a glass of water."

"Sure, I'll be right back," she said, glancing at Jordan. Jordan nodded and then turned to watch her walk away.

"And who do we have here?" Camille asked.

"Jordan," Mamma Lou said, looking up and

smiling. "You came. I'm so happy. I hoped you could make it."

"Actually I've been here for some time. I apologize for not finding you earlier. I was talking to your grandson Tony and his wife, Madison. They're a great couple. I'll be stopping by his antique store tomorrow. I also met Kennedy, Juwan, Raymond and Hope."

"Oh, good. It sounds like you've been having a wonderful time."

"Yes, I have. Thank you so much for inviting me." Louise turned and smiled at the woman sitting beside her. The woman smiled back attentively. "Jordan, I'd like to introduce you to a very dear friend of mine and a very special woman, Camille Rantone. Camille, this is Jordan Hamilton."

He stepped forward and extended his hand, taking hers gently. "Ma'am, it's a pleasure to meet you. I'm sorry I missed the beginning of your story. It sounded fascinating. I'd love to hear the whole thing one of these days."

"Thank you, Jordan, and I wouldn't worry too much about missing the beginning of the story. We'll have plenty of time to chat real soon."

Jordan looked at her oddly. He wasn't sure what she meant. Still, he was immediately impressed by her warmth and gentleness. There was something about her engaging manner that warmed him as soon as he touched her hand. She kept holding his hand and smiled looking directly into his eyes. "Jordan Hamilton, it's truly a pleasure to meet you. You're a creator, a man who works with his hands. That's a very honorable profession."

"Yes, ma'am, I do work with my hands. I'm an architect and a builder," Jordan said.

"Actually, I see you are much more than that. You have an old soul, Jordan Hamilton. That's a very good thing."

"You see?" Jordan repeated, glancing at Mamma Lou.

"Camille is a clairvoyant."

"Really?" he said, smiling at Camille again.

"Sometimes yes and sometimes not so much," Camille said. "You, not so much. But I see you have an open mind. That's good, very good. I've been waiting a long time for you."

"You have?" he asked inquisitively.

"Camille, Jordan is one of the owners of Hamilton Development. His company is building a resort out on Crescent Point."

"Oh, how wonderful. It's about time someone found something to do with that plot of land. And you are the perfect man to take care of the property. You will learn to care for this land. You'll know exactly what to do. You know there was a large fishing company there many years ago."

"That's right, I was told that when we bought the land."

"So, are you enjoying your time on the island, Jordan? I hope you're getting out and meeting people," Mamma Lou said.

"Actually, I don't stay on the island that much."

"Now that's a shame. May I ask why?" Camille said.

"Right now my workload varies. Most days it takes me back to our main office outside of D.C."

"What about weekends?" she asked.

"Especially on weekends," he confirmed.

"Then you're missing the best part of the island. There are so many things for young people to do."

Sheri returned. "Sorry it took so long," Sheri said, placing a glass on the small table beside Camille's chair. She turned to Jordan and smiled pleasantly. "Grandma, did you meet Jordan?"

"Yes, we just met." She winked. "I think he's a keeper." Louise nodded in agreement.

"Thank you, ladies. Mamma Lou, thank you for a wonderful evening. I had a great time. I'm gonna head out now."

"You're very welcome. Make sure you come visit me again."

"I will," he promised.

"Good night, ladies."

"Sheri, be a dear and walk Jordan out. Thank you."

She nodded and led the way to the front door.

He opened it and they stepped outside. They walked down the path. "How long have you known Mamma Lou?" he asked.

"All my life," she said. "She and my grandmother are best friends. They met over sixty years ago."

"They look dangerous."

She laughed. "You have no idea. They've been trying to match me up for the past two years."

"And?" he asked curiously.

"And nothing. I guess I'm a one-date kind of woman."

"I hope that's not true."

"Since you and I have never actually been out on a date," she said, "you don't have anything to worry about right now."

"How about we rectify that. Would you like to go out with me tomorrow?"

Sheri smiled and nodded. "Yes. I'd like that."

"Good, it's a date." They got to his truck and stopped.

"You do know there's no ferry this late, right."

"My brothers and I rent a condo at the Crescent Regency. How late are you staying tonight?" he asked.

"Not long, probably another half hour or so, why?"

"I'll see you later." He got into his truck and drove away.

* * *

Louise and Camille watched through the front window. Louise gripped Camille's hand and nodded. Camille smiled. It was exactly what she wanted to see. "Yes, he's perfect, thank you, Louise."

Chapter 16

Sheri left the party an hour later. She drove home, showered, then changed into a T-shirt and boxers. She lay down across the bed and checked her messages before turning in for the night. There were five new messages including one text from Jordan Hamilton. I'm hungry. She read it, smiled and then typed a simple reply. What do you want to eat? She went on to the next five emails. Just as she saved the last one, her cell phone vibrated. It was another message from Jordan. You! She typed in her reply then closed her phone, rolled onto her back and looked up at the ceiling fan above her bed. It was a good night.

They had danced, they had talked and it was wonderful. She knew in her heart it was happening so fast. But she couldn't stop it. She was already there—in love with a man who was impossible to love. She knew her heart would be broken and that it was only a matter of time, but she opened up anyway. Mama Lou was right all those months ago when she first introduced them. Jordan Hamilton was the man for her. She just wasn't the woman for him.

She shook her head and chuckled, thinking about Jordan's last text message and her reply. Bon appétit. He was incorrigible and she was definitely playing with fire and knew it. He was dangerous to her heart. They wanted two different things and there was no way their differences could ever be resolved. But while she had him, she intended to enjoy every minute of it.

She sighed heavily and closed her eyes. A second later her cell phone rang. She looked over at the alarm clock on the bedside table. It was just after midnight. She figured it was either Kennedy, Madison or her mother calling so she picked up. "Hello."

"Are you in bed?"

She immediately recognized Jordan's voice. "Uh-huh."

"Perfect. It's after midnight," he said.

"Uh-huh," she confirmed, curious as to why he was calling her.

"That makes it officially tomorrow. Technically we could be on our date."

"Uh-huh."

"Feel like coming out to play?"

"No, not really," she said. "I feel like staying in."

"I thought you'd never ask."

A split second later her doorbell rang. She sat up. Her heart raced as she nearly had a panic attack. "Is that you?"

"Uh-huh. I told you I was hungry."

She got up and looked at herself in the mirror. What was she doing? This was crazy. But she couldn't stop herself. Maybe he was right. Maybe there was some unseen force pulling them together. She went to the door and opened it. Jordan was standing there with a large box in his hands. He had changed clothes from the stylish business suit he'd worn earlier at the party to a pair of casual pants and a button-down shirt. She looked at the box in his hands. "Flowers would have been nicer," she said.

"I thought you might appreciate this better. May I?"

"Sure, come in." She stepped aside. He walked in. He placed the box beside her sofa and then turned. She watched as his eyes flowed over her body. She liked the way he reacted to seeing her. She grazed her teeth across her lower lip, a habit that Jordan found very seductive, as she walked over to him and started unbuttoning his shirt. When it was opened, she pushed it back over his shoulders and it dropped to the floor. She couldn't help touching him. His chest was wide and magnificent. Her hands roamed his body of their own accord. She pushed him back so that he was leaning against the door and began unzipping his pants. She reached down and felt his solid body, which was already hard for her. A ripple of excitement shot through her. She kissed his chest and licked his nipples, touching and feeling him everywhere. *Bon appétit.*

When she stopped she saw that his breathing was rough and ragged and his eyes were flooded with passion. She reached down the front of his pants again, but this time he grabbed her hands and stopped her. "We have all night and I want every inch of you."

She smirked. "I don't know. Can you handle me all night?"

"Don't challenge me. It's not a good idea right now."

She smiled slyly, staring directly into his dark sexy eyes. "Well, then, by all means, consider yourself challenged."

He grabbed her and kissed her nearly senseless. His lips were firm and intense, ravaging her mouth and unsettling her mind. He had her hemmed in with no possible escape and she loved it. She surrendered willingly. When he finally leaned back, she heard a low groan emanating from his throat. "I am hungry. I've wanted to taste you all night long," he whispered. He kissed her again, pinning her back against the door just as she had earlier. His kiss was passionate and powerful as he held her in a viselike grip. She couldn't move even if she wanted to. She closed her eyes and wrapped her arms around his neck. In the next moment, he picked her up and carried her to another room. When she opened her eyes she was in her bedroom. He lowered her to the floor and stepped back.

He pulled her T-shirt over her head and looked down at her skimpy shorts, shaking his head. He sat down on the side of the bed and pulled her closer so that she stood between his legs. "Turn around."

She obeyed. His hands were on her hips, massaging them from the front and back. He turned her around and looked up at her. Never breaking eye contact, he pulled the shorts down and smiled as he licked his lips. He gestured for her to sit beside him and lie back on the bed. She did. He began kissing her lips and her neck as his hands stroked and caressed her breasts. Her thoughts seemed to vanish. She could barely keep up with the onslaught of his hands as they probed her body.

Then she felt his hand between her legs and his fingers delve deep inside her. Her body shook as her wetness covered him. He seemed to delight in her body's offering. His kisses trailed lower along the length of her body. He licked and suckled her breasts. His torturous mouth and tongue were setting her body on fire as he moved lower and lower and lower. When he got to her stomach he opened her legs wider and began stroking her peak of pleasure. She writhed in sexual agony. Then Jordan dropped to his knees and wedged his body between her legs. He pulled her to the edge of the bed and draped her legs over his shoulders. She gasped. He maneuvered so quickly she barely registered what had happened.

He spread her legs wider to gain better access to her well-lubricated opening and took one long luscious lick as if she were a lollipop. "*Bon appétit,* indeed." He licked her again. Her legs trembled and her heart almost stopped. She felt jittery and dizzy. Then he devoured her. Her body reacted by arching upward off the bed. He was gentle and thorough as he held her legs and feasted like a starving man. Her breathing became panting. Her mind became mush. She screamed her pleasure and then she exploded. That's all she remembered.

Sheri opened her eyes slowly. Jordan was sitting on the side of the bed looking down at her with a concerned expression on his face.

"Hey, welcome back," he said softly, caressing her face.

"What was that? What happened?" she asked.

"I have no idea. But I think you fainted. Are you okay?"

"Yeah, fine. I've never fainted before. That was intense. How long was I out?"

"Not long, about a minute. Sheri, I didn't mean to…"

She sat up. "I'm fine, really." She looked down at his body. He still had his pants on, but she could see the outline of his erection pressed against his crotch. He was still rock hard. She reached down to stroke him. His body twitched. "One of us is way too overdressed."

He smiled. "That would be me," he said.

She nodded. He stood up and removed his pants and boxer briefs, then grabbed a condom and covered himself. "Are you sure?"

"Oh, yeah, baby. Positive. Come here," she beckoned, lying back on the pillows at the top of the bed. He climbed back onto the bed and hovered over her a moment then slowly eased himself into her. Once he had entered her, he propelled his shaft with a deep thrust, filling her completely. Then he pulled out and plunged in again. Each time the pace increased. Breathless and panting, their bodies met passion for passion, plunging deeper and deeper. He pumped and she held tight. Again and again, deeper and deeper they ravaged each other until their union exploded in a mind-blowing, earth-shattering climax. Clench. Fill. Release. The intensity of the experience overwhelmed them as they collapsed on the bed, their bodies spent—but only for a short time.

All night long meant twice more in bed and again as they showered together. By dawn they had used all of the condoms. They slept cuddled together still feeling the afterglow of sexual ecstasy.

Chapter 17

Their second night together was beyond amazing. Sheri still couldn't believe she'd fainted. As usual she woke up just before her alarm went off. She reached over and turned it off then gazed down at the man in her bed. She smiled. He was still asleep and he was gorgeous. After they'd made love the last time, she could see he was exhausted. She was on top. When they finally achieved sexual rapture, she collapsed on his chest and they both fell asleep. Now, there was no way she was going to wake him up. She showered, dressed, left a note for him to join her later, made a pot of coffee and went to work.

Saturdays at the museum were usually busy.

Sheri arrived early, knowing it was going to be crazy. Jordan called twice, but she missed both calls and didn't have time to call him back. By late morning, the activities of the day had been a complete blur. The museum was crowded from morning to early afternoon. There were four busloads of visitors, a Girl Scout troop and a senior-citizens group. Add to that, three docents called in sick. Sheri was happy to pitch in and help give tours, but this certainly wasn't what she'd planned to do all morning.

She welcomed the Girl Scout troop at the front entrance and escorted them to the main exhibit area. She introduced herself and asked if anyone had been to the museum before or had questions before the tour started. With no replies she began the tour in the main exhibit hall. She showed them pictures of the *Mabella Louisa* and gave them a general idea of events at the time the ship was sea-going.

The Girl Scouts were interested for the most part. But as the tour wound down, she noticed the group had become extremely quiet and reserved. She opened one of the glass cases and demonstrated the workings of some of the artifacts. She allowed a couple of the girls to come up and touch the items.

"What is it?"

"It's a cannonball," Sheri said.

"Aren't they supposed to be bigger?"

"Actually this one is a lot heavier than it appears. This kind was specifically designed to attack smaller ships at close range. Would anyone like to hold it?" Every one of the scouts raised their hands. Some even jumped eagerly. Sheri smiled and waded through the throng of now eager listeners. A short while later she put the ball back in its case. The girls were astonished to feel how heavy a cannonball was. After that the questions flowed like water.

Several girls wanted to know if she got to play with any of the items in the display cases and others wanted to know how long it took to collect everything.

"That's a good question," she responded. She explained that as a historian she was mainly responsible for authenticating the museum's collections and keeping them in as good a condition as possible. She talked about all the records she kept and relayed several stories from journals and diaries she'd read. They loved the stories about everyday life on Crescent Island, and how as a new settlement the inhabitants lived and defended their land.

"The museum's collections are comprised of borrowed and donated items, as well as gifts from patrons. We have over five thousand artistic, cultural and historical items found both here on Crescent Island and also on mainland Virginia. Our goal is to promote educational awareness through these collections and many others."

"How do you borrow the items? Is it like a library and anybody can borrow them?"

"That's a good question. No. Not everyone can borrow items in the museum's collections because they're very special to our history. It's a very long and complicated process to borrow something from us. This is a small museum and if we lent out everything we'd have nothing to show you when you visit. So we are very particular about what artifacts we lend."

"So do you own everything here?"

"Actually some of the exhibits do belong to the museum. What you saw in the main exhibit hall, the *Mabella Louisa,* is an example of a permanent exhibit that belongs to this museum. In reality it is on permanent loan. The pieces of the ship were found and donated by a very brilliant and generous man. His name was Nicholas Rantone. He was my great-grandfather."

"How did he find the items?"

Sheri turned and looked up toward the back of the exhibit, as did everyone else in the small group. Jordan stood leaning against a wall looking at her. "Good afternoon," she said. "Welcome. I'm glad you came."

There was a hush as the girls began to giggle and look from Jordan to Sheri excitedly. "To answer your question, Nicholas Rantone's family came to this island shortly after it was settled in 1868. His family bought land and, as a teenager, he started collecting the things he found on the beach and at the inlet. That collection grew to become very large—too large to just keep in an old shed.

"He went to his good friend, Jonah Gates, a member of one of the founding families. They went to the city leaders and proposed building a structure to house the collection. The city officials agreed. Nicholas built it here on this site that became the museum. He brought everything he'd collected over the years and displayed the items for everyone to see. Jonah contributed his family heirlooms as well. Those original pieces were the beginning of this island's museum and the basis for its history."

She saw Jordan nodding his head. She hoped that he was finally beginning to understand the importance of collecting and keeping Crescent Island's history.

"Do you get stuff from other museums?"

"Yes, sometimes we request parts of exhibits from other museums. It's an exchange. We borrow and we lend. That way everyone gets to see and experience the treasures of the past."

"What kind of treasures?"

She smiled happily. "There are all kinds of treasure, some more valuable in people's eyes than gold and silver. Yes, we do have coins and jewels, but more importantly we have history. Are there any more questions?" she asked, looking around.

"Yes, I have another question. Do you enjoy being an historian?"

"Yes, I do, very much. Okay, perhaps we'd better continue with our tour." Sheri spent the next forty-five minutes walking the museum and telling the Girl Scouts about the various exhibits and displays. She glanced up from time to time to see Jordan watching her attentively. When the tour ended and the group arrived back at the main floor she thanked them and invited them to come again soon. They cheered and applauded.

As soon as they left she looked around for Jordan. She found him in the main exhibit hall reading the ship's manifesto from the *Mabella Louisa* exhibit. She walked over to him. "Welcome again. Thank you for coming." she whispered.

He turned to her. "I'm enjoying the exhibit. Your talk was very enlightening. Nicholas was your great-grandfather?" She nodded. "So history does run in your family. Nicholas was the original builder and founder and your grandmother is a folklorist and clairvoyant."

"Yes. I am very connected to this place. Most of the items are found in various sites around the island. They're still being found."

He looked up and around the building. "I walked

around the building before I joined your tour group. It's very old and very decrepit," he said softly.

"Maybe a little," she confessed.

"No, maybe a lot," he said firmly. "The lighting system downstairs flickers and the heating and air-conditioning systems are completely shot. The foundation is crumbling and I don't even want to discuss the fire code violations."

"Sometimes it seems the building is falling down on our heads, literally. But it's all we have to keep the history of this island alive."

"You need more."

"Maybe one day," she said wistfully. Sheri watched Jordan as he strolled around the exhibit hall. "Find this interesting?" she said hopefully.

He nodded. "What exactly is an S-U-R?"

"An S-U-R is a ship of unknown registry. In the case of the *Mabella Louisa* it was a merchant ship lost in the late eighteen hundreds. It was sold after the Civil War to abolitionists and given to freedmen hoping to go back to their families in Africa. Unfortunately the ship was old and worthless. The people who sold it knew it would barely leave the harbor. But it did. The freedmen sailed down the bay and that's where the vessel began to take on water. Fearing for their lives they headed to the closest landmass, Crescent Island. This is where they landed."

"The ship sank off the coast?"

"Later, yes," said Sheri.

"And what about the *Crescent?*" Jordan asked.

"The *Crescent* was the sister ship. It left later. Historians believe it made it to Africa."

"You don't believe that, do you?" Jordan said.

"No. I believe it sank off Crescent Point. The search for ships that were part of the American Colonization Society's repatriation movement— where freed slaves returned to Africa and formed the country of Liberia—is practically nonexistent since most shipwreck dive searches are looking for lost treasure. There wasn't a lot of treasure on a ship carrying freed slaves."

"Why is the *Crescent* so important?"

"It's history. It's our history—every man, woman and child on this island and in this country." She looked over as the group of seniors arrived. "I have another tour to give."

"Mind if I tag along?"

"Yes."

He smiled. She knew he was going to accompany the group anyway. She began the tour the same way, with the same exhibit, but everything else was different. She engaged the elderly museum goers more and they loved it. When the tour ended forty minutes later, she walked them to the museum entrance and returned to see Jordan still standing behind her.

"Thank you for the tour. It was enlightening."

"Are you going to hang around town this weekend?" she asked.

"Yes, I'm gonna stop by Tony Gates's antique shop."

She smiled. "Okay, see you later. Tell Tony I said hi."

"Tony and Raymond are friends of yours?" he asked.

"They're like my big brothers. We all grew up and hung out together. My brothers Daniel and Mark are their best friends. I was the pesky little sister that constantly tattled on them."

He nodded. "See you later."

Sheri walked him to the museum exit and went back to her office. She still had a full day ahead of her.

Jordan grabbed a small box from his trunk and walked down the street toward the center of town. He crossed when he saw the antique shop up ahead. Gates Antiques Limited was actually two redbrick buildings side by side. One was a gallery for local artists and artisans, and the other was an antique shop. Both were a lot bigger and busier than he'd expected. He opened the door and walked in. A large man with thick muscles, a beer belly and a receding hairline looked up and greeted him. He sat behind the front counter with his eyes glued to a computer monitor. The other people in the shop were already being helped, so he walked over to the hefty man.

"Welcome to Crescent Island. Jerry Duncan, store manager. How can I help you today?" he said.

"Is Tony Gates around?"

"Hold on, let me check." He picked up the phone and asked the person on the other end about Tony's whereabouts. He nodded and hung up. "Tony will be right down. Have a look around while you're waiting."

"Thanks." Jordan did just that. He was astounded by the collection of gems, precious stones, coins and well-preserved nineteenth-century-era artifacts. Each item seemed to have a unique story and historical value attached to it. Some items were so rare they weren't for sale. One in particular caught his eye. It was a simple gold band with a cluster of red stones on top sitting in a small wooden box. Jordan leaned down to read the small card. The box was called Sheba.

Tony walked up and stood beside Jordan. "Stunning, isn't it?" he said, looking at the precious gem in the display case. He smiled knowingly.

Jordan turned and extended his hand. The two men shook and greeted each other. Tony welcomed Jordan to his shop. Jordan turned back to the beautiful treasure. "This is gorgeous."

Tony nodded. "Yes, it is."

"Where did you find it?"

"I was in North Africa on a buying trip and I visited an old Moorish monastery on the border of Morocco and Algeria. The land was sold to a developer. It was about to be demolished and everything had to be sold. I met with the caretaker of the monastery. We talked and I saw the things he had for sale. I purchased everything, including the iron gates to the monastery. But this I found just sitting on a shelf. I opened it and discovered an old ring encrusted with dirt. I could barely make out the design, but I knew it was the real thing. The caretaker told me that the ring was given to the Queen of Sheba by King Solomon in biblical times."

"Wait, you mean *the* Queen of Sheba and *the* King Solomon?"

Tony nodded. "I know, I thought the same thing. The man had to be crazy or something. Still, I bought it anyway and had it authenticated by a friend at the Metropolitan Museum of Art in New York. The results were astonishing. They identified the type of metal and the wooden box it came in and my jaw dropped."

Jordan looked back at the case. "What is it?"

"They checked, double-checked and then triple-checked. The wood is called almug. It's been extinct now for over two thousand years and was primarily indigenous to Middle Eastern countries. The almug tree is mentioned in the Old Testament and is believed to have been used in building Solomon's Temple. The Metropolitan Museum made an offer for it."

"You didn't sell it or donate it?"

"It's no longer mine. I gave it to my wife on our wedding day. Her sister, Kennedy, and Sheri handle loaning it out for her. This is an exact replica. The real Sheba ring and box is on loan to the Met."

Jordan just shook his head. "Man, that's unreal."

Tony looked at the Sheba. "It's history."

"So wait, how in the world did this ring and box get to a monastery in North Africa?"

Tony chuckled. "Yeah, I forgot to tell you that one—it's a long story. The caretaker told me that after Sheba left Israel to go home, King Solomon put the ring in this box and gave it to her. It was then passed down through countless generations, lost and stolen many, many times. Then he said one day an old, sick woman went to the monastery for help. She died. But before she died she gave the monks the box that had been in her family for centuries. She was the last in her family's line."

"That story is serious."

"It's still amazing to me. So, what's in the box?"

"That's what I need you to tell me," Jordan said.

"Come up to the office and I'll have a look."

Then two men went upstairs to Tony's office. Jordan stopped in the doorway as Tony continued to his work desk. "Wow," Jordan said as he looked around. "This room is incredible. Is that what I think it is?" Jordan asked as he spied what looked like a small sarcophagus on a worktable.

Tony chuckled. "Yep. It's headed to auction at my gallery in Alexandria. Have a seat."

Jordan sat down, opened the box and pulled out the bell found at the site. Tony draped a cloth over his worktable and adjusted the overhead light. He grabbed a pair of plastic gloves and picked it up. Using a brush, he dusted some of the loose dirt away. "Where'd you find this?"

"My company is doing construction at Crescent Point."

"That's a great plot of land out there. How's the project going?"

"The main structure is complete, just cosmetics at this point. We're about to start on the secondary site hopefully this coming week. That's where this was discovered."

Tony asked a few more questions as he continued working on the bell. Jordan told him about his other projects and his brothers and how they took over their father's company to fulfill his dream. After a while Jordan stopped talking as Tony continued working. Jordan went back downstairs and looked around. About an hour later Jerry walked over to Jordan.

"Tony wants you to come to the office."

Jordan nodded and headed back upstairs. Tony was in his office on the phone. He motioned for

Jordan to come in. A few minutes later he hung up. "Okay, it looks like you have a piece of history here. I just called and confirmed a few tests. Of course there will be a lot more if you choose to pursue this, but in my opinion, this is the original bell from the *Crescent*."

"I know the general history of the island. But can you tell me more about the actual ship?" said Jordan.

"That would be Sheri's department. She's the foremost expert on the *Crescent* and the *Mabella Louisa* and just about everything about the history of the island," said Tony.

"That might be a problem."

"May I ask why? It seemed to me that the two of you had some pretty serious chemistry going on last night at the party."

Jordan smiled and shook his head. "She's amazing. I hate to say this and I swear I'd deny ever uttering the words, but Mamma Lou got it right. She is incredible."

Tony nodded. "Yes. So why can't you talk to Sheri about what you found?"

"She wants to close the site down. I have a deadline and a lot of money, not to mention all the men and women working out there who are depending on me for their jobs for the next month or so."

"I see your point."

"I can't tell her, not yet. I dropped a box off to

her last night with some less important artifacts. If she knew about this bell…"

"I understand. I won't say anything. It's not my place. But my advice is to tell her before this gets out of hand. Sheri takes the preservation of Crescent Island history very seriously. She shouldn't find out another way," Tony advised.

Jordan nodded as Tony put the bell in a more secure enclosure with his label on it. "Thanks for everything." They shook hands. Jordan left with his box and some things he'd purchased downstairs while he had been waiting. He got into his truck and headed for the condo. He had some serious thinking to do. Back in his condo, he sat at his drawing table and began sketching. The next two hours flew by in a flash.

Chapter 18

Sheri left the job early. It was almost two o'clock in the afternoon, and busy or not she was on a more important mission. Jordan needed to learn to appreciate history, her history. She made a few phone calls then went back home, changed and headed over to her mother's inn.

"Wow, look at you. You look sensational. Who's the lucky—" Lois stopped midsentence and smiled. "Well, it's about time you listened to your mother. What are you going to do this afternoon?"

"I thought I'd take Jordan Hamilton for a tour of the island and then have a late dinner at Colonel Wheeler's place."

"Perfect, that sounds perfect. What do you need?"

Sheri told her mother her plans in detail and Lois, the consummate host and gourmet, came up with some wonderful ideas. Fifteen minutes later, Sheri grabbed her motorcycle and headed to the Regency condos. She leaned back, removed her helmet, pulled out her cell phone and called the phone number from the night before. Jordan answered.

"Hey, let's go."

"Go where?" he asked.

"To see Crescent Island."

"Where are you?"

"Out front. Come on, let's go."

A few minutes later she saw Jordan in her rear-view mirror. He looked up and down the street then stopped and stared at her from behind. He smiled and walked over.

"I'd know that body anywhere. A motorcycle?"

"Grab the helmet and get on." She put her helmet back on, felt the snugness of his body pressed behind her and took off. They started at one end of the island and worked their way to the other. They stopped at the highest peak on the island and looked down on the landscape below. The view was sensational.

"It's beautiful," Jordan said.

"Yes, it is. I love it here. Crescent Island's local

economy is based on tourism. It's the main attraction. While other islands in the Chesapeake Bay suffered during the downturn in the economy, we thrived." She pointed out some of the more popular tourist attractions and told him a bit of local history, along with some of the native legends and folklore.

"A lighthouse?" Jordan said, seeing the stark white, tall, conical-shaped, two-story structure on the edge of the coastline. "That's near the point."

"Yes, it is."

"Does anyone live there?"

"Yes, Mamma Lou's fiancé, Colonel Wheeler. The lighthouse is separate from his living quarters and is completely renovated in a sort of rustic decor. There's a bay window that overlooks the cliffs and out onto the bay. It's beautiful and the lighthouse still works. It's about two hundred years old and was declared a landmark a few years back. It was used to protect the Eastern Shore against the British during the Revolutionary War.

"But one of the most popular tourist sites is the old slaves' cemetery and the freed slaves' shantytown. It's right over there. The shantytown was a small, insular community on the northernmost far side of the island near the harbor inlet."

"Can we go?"

"Sure." She drove about twenty minutes then pulled up to a small outcropping of buildings in a secluded area on the side of the road. She stopped.

Jordan got off the motorcycle, and Sheri followed. He walked toward the large sign and read it.

By 1863, when the Emancipation Proclamation became law, several hundred newly freed slaves boarded shipping vessels supplied by abolitionists and sailed east hoping to get back to Africa. Instead they landed on these shores and settled here. Brought by the *Mabella Louisa* and the *Crescent,* this was their home.

"What a wonderful history. It's so beautiful here. I can see why you love it so much."

He continued walking toward the small shanty-town. Sheri followed quietly behind him. Jordan walked in and out of the old wooden structures that the freed slaves called home more than a hundred years ago. He walked up the few steps to enter a small building once home to a family of freed slaves. "Wow, this is amazing."

"The museum and historical society take great pride in this site, and have gone to great lengths to care for it and to keep the past as true as possible," Sheri said in a soft, reverential tone.

"You mentioned that your great-grandfather came later. Are there any direct descendants of the freed slaves still on the island?"

"Yes, you met some last night. The Gates family members are original descendants. Mamma Lou married Jonathan Gates. His ancestor was Jonah, a freed slave and one of the original settlers."

"Amazing," he whispered.

Sheri smiled. Maybe she was getting through to him. "Come, I want to show you one other place."

They got back on the bike and rode along narrow roads through the outer banks of the island. The view was spectacular. The sky was clear and the air smelled of seawater and fresh flowers. After fifteen minutes they turned into a small parking area.

"This is the first established church on the island. It was designated a national historic site and completely restored years ago." Jordan headed toward the building, but there were already a lot of people there. "Wait, this way," Sheri said.

They walked around the side of the church and passed through an old wooden gate that led to a century-old cemetery. "There are a lot of anonymous heroes buried here. We know about Frederick Douglass and Harriet Tubman, but there were others, dozens who fought for freedom. Their names will never be known."

They walked among the old headstones, lost in their own thoughts. The moment was still and peaceful.

Jordan stopped and read one of the headstones. "'Here lies Anne Louise Black, 1860-1880, Beloved daughter, wife and mother.'"

"I love this stone. It reminds me of the preciousness of life. Anne Louise was only twenty when she died in childbirth. She was a slave for a good part of her life. Her mother taught her to read and write and her father was killed during the Civil War. She had three sisters, who she never saw again. She was on board the *Crescent* when it sank, losing everything she had. Everyone survived. She swam and found a new life."

"How do you know all that?" he asked.

"I have her diary. I just wish I had more. I wish I knew more. She's like an unfinished story, but at least she died free," she said, in barely a whisper.

Jordan took her hand and suddenly felt the joy of seeing Sheri's world and experiencing her history. They walked back to the church. The tourists were all gone. They climbed the four wooden steps and entered the small wooden shack. It was like they'd stepped back in time. They walked the short distance to the front of the church. The windowless area inside was narrow. There was a small altar atop a one-step rising. Twenty or thirty backless benches ran along either side of the center aisle. The floor was bare wooden planks with large rusty nails hammered solidly in place. There was the slightest coat of dust on the floor that seemed to belong there.

Jordan looked into Sheri's hopeful eyes.

"I understand," he said, barely above a whisper.

She nodded realizing that the tour had conveyed her love of the island and given Jordan a new insight into the value of the few artifacts unearthed at Crescent Point. She had succeeded.

"Let's go. We have dinner reservations."

They went back outside just as a small van pulled up and unloaded dozens of excited tourists. "Hey," he said. "Give me the keys." She tossed them to him. He climbed on the bike and started the engine. She nodded, impressed, grabbed her helmet and put it on. Moments later they were headed back into town.

The splendor of Saturday's late-afternoon adventure turned into Saturday evening's midnight love. Jordan changed and picked Sheri up in his truck. They ordered takeout from Colonel Wheeler's seafood restaurant and ate dinner on the balcony of Jordan's condo. The view from his terrace took in the northern shore of the island toward the heart of the bay. The lights in the distance twinkled and shimmered, matching the stars that shone down from above. The sight was breathtaking. They sat outside after dinner and talked about their childhoods, and dreams of the future. Neither dared mention anything beyond that moment.

Afterward they headed to the inn for dessert. A sampling of the house specialty desserts was the perfect ending to a spectacular day. Lois welcomed them with a basket already packed and ready for takeout. They ate outside on the balcony of the inn.

The view from the hill where the inn was perched was of the town below. The stars shining down were just as breathtaking. Beyond the town was the bay. They ate, laughed and watched the boats sail the midnight waters. A slightly chilly breeze teased around them. Sheri wrapped her arms around her body.

Jordan encircled her body with his arms, pulling and holding her close. "Thank you for today," he whispered in her ear.

"You're welcome."

They stared out into the still, peaceful night. The moment was perfect. She had to know. He kissed her neck then turned her around, tipped her chin up and looked into her soft brown eyes.

"When I came here months ago I saw Crescent Island as just another location, a place to build then just move on. It's been the story of my life even with relationships. I rest for a moment then move on. I never saw myself ever staying long enough to fall in love. To be loved."

"And now?"

He smiled. "And then there's you. There's you and I can't stop thinking about you. Mamma Lou was right. You are the one for me. And I knew it as soon as I saw you months ago. But I refused to accept it, to open my heart. I love you, Sheri. I have since the moment I saw you. You don't have to say anything. I just want you to know how I feel."

She smiled, her eyes nearly brimming with tears. "Jordan, I love you, too." They kissed gently and tenderly, sealing their love with an embrace that would last forever.

I love you, he mouthed silently.

"I love you, too."

"Feel like getting married?"

She stopped just as her heart jumped. "What?"

"Will you marry me?" His cell phone rang. He frowned. "Talk about horrible timing, I need to get this. It's only for emergencies."

Sheri waited as Jordan answered his cell phone in the other room. She heard him talking.

"This had better be good," he warned. Moments later he came out, obviously distressed. "I have to go. We'll talk when I get back."

"Everything okay?" Sheri asked.

"I'm not sure." He kissed her, smiled and hurried out. From the balcony she watched him run to his truck and drive away. His rear lights disappeared down the street toward town. She went back inside, closed the door and went to bed. Knowing he'd call and join her there. Then she'd answer his question. "Yes."

Jordan called Cleveland back as soon as he got into his truck. It wasn't that he didn't want to talk in front of Sheri, he just didn't want to waste time getting there. "Okay, I'm on my way. What's going on exactly?"

"One of the employees decided it would be a good idea to post information online about what we've found out here. I saw the post. It says we have a treasure chest filled with money and gold coins. They directed everyone to the main building on the opposite side of the site. We've had fools climbing the fences trespassing all evening. We've got some damage. I already called the authorities. They've been here the past half hour."

"Good, anybody hurt?"

"Nah, not really, although we put a hell of a scare into a few of them, before they lit out of here. But I don't think it's the end of it. Damn movies! Everybody thinks they're a pirate looking for lost treasure now. We did catch one of the main culprits or rather he got caught himself. He didn't know I put the cameras up like we discussed. He did all this as a distraction. While we were chasing trespassers all night, he apparently intended to have the secondary site all to himself. We caught him red-handed, so to speak." He chuckled.

"It's Jamie, the new kid. He climbed the back fence with someone else and they started digging. Then he hopped up on the backhoe thinking he knew what he was doing. He didn't. He cracked the arm again. It toppled over. He fell in the hole trapped by the machine." Cleveland chuckled again. "It's not funny, I know, but man, there was mud everywhere. It took three of us to get his slippery, slimy butt out of there. Another sheriff's deputy just pulled up. Oh, and get this, he wants his daddy."

"I'm turning in now. I'll be there in a few seconds."

"Jordan, one more thing, in the process of trying to climb out this half-wit dug up what looks like an anchor and a chest."

"I'm here." Jordan parked and ran to the secondary site. Cleveland stood talking to the local sheriff and two other security guards, who were holding a very pissed off Jamie at arm's length. One was chuckling, the other was near hysterics. Between them, Jamie was covered head to toe in mud. Jordan approached, shaking his head. The sight would have been funny if it weren't so serious.

Cleveland saw Jordan and walked over with the sheriff. They explained the next step. Apparently, Jamie was the one causing all the trouble on-site. He was angry that his father's company didn't get the job, and instead his father made him work. Jordan realized it was going to be a long night. He called his brothers and told them what had happened and what had been found. Then he left a message another. "Kenneth, it's Jordan, call me ASAP."

Cleveland handed Jordan a sealed envelope. "What's this?"

"The kid had it on him. He said it was his, but I doubt his name is Anne Louise Black."

"Anne," Jordan said softly. He opened the envelope and pulled out the book. He smiled. It was another diary. "Maybe Anne's story will have a happy ending after all."

"They're taking him in now," Cleveland said. "What do you want to do with this other stuff?"

He grabbed his keys from his pocket and handed them to Cleveland. "We're shipping it out tonight."

Cleveland nodded and turned to the other security guards. "You, let's go. We have work to do."

Jordan put the book back in the envelope. He couldn't wait to give it to Sheri.

Chapter 19

"It *is* the *Crescent*. They knew and you're not going to believe what happened," Genie said, rushing into Sheri's office like a tornado on caffeine and a six-pack of energy drinks. Her eyes were wide and she was breathless.

Sheri looked up. "Oh, my God, Genie! What's wrong?"

"It's Jamie, they took him in."

"What? Who took him in?" she asked, trying to calm her down.

"He had Jamie arrested last night! His father is furious. I know he's gonna kill him. He's on the board of supervisors and all. But still they can kill people, too, right?"

"Genie, stop! Slow down and tell me what's going on?"

"Late last night Jamie and I went to Crescent Point and found a chest and an anchor on the construction site."

"You did what?" Sheri nearly shrieked.

"We thought we could just get everything out instead of dealing with all the red tape. We were there before and we tried, but this time we were ready. We thought it would be easy. Then I could be famous and get a job in D.C."

"Genie, Lord, what have you done?" she said.

"Nothing, nothing. We didn't do anything. We dug and found an anchor and a chest. But then the machine fell on top of Jamie and he got caught in the hole. Now he's in jail. I can't believe he got arrested. But they knew about it all along. Why else would they have those cameras and stuff? They knew."

"What? Who knew?"

"Jordan Hamilton knew about the *Crescent* all along. He had the site closed off because he knew what was up there. It's what was breaking the backhoe all those times before—the anchor."

"No, that's impossible. He couldn't know."

Genie nodded her head rapidly. "That's what Jamie said and he was right. I saw it. It's there."

"The anchor and a chest? Where are they now?"

"I watched for a little while until after the sheriff took Jamie away. They pulled it out and loaded it up in Hamilton's truck. I don't know where they took it. It's probably in the trash by now."

"Genie, listen to me. You need to talk to your mother and father about what happened last night. Then you need to have them take you to the sheriff. You need to get in front of this before it blows up in your face."

"I know," she said. "Jamie kept saying it was my fault. I can't believe he told on me like that. I just came in because I wanted you to know what really happened. It really is the *Crescent*."

She nodded. "I know. Okay, I asked nicely. Now it's time to go in another direction. He mentioned a court order before. I think that's exactly what I need to get to stop him."

"How are you going to get a court order in time to stop them from digging up that whole area? It takes days, maybe weeks to get one, right?"

"No, not always, I have enough lawyers in my family to know that. There's something called an emergency injunction. It's probably only going to be temporary, but it should give me enough time to get some of the artifacts and have them analyzed. Then I can make my assessment and go from there."

"Who do you know who can get a court order fast?"

"I'm going to ask my great-uncle. He's a Virginia circuit court judge."

"What if your uncle doesn't give you a court order?"

"Then I'll think of something else," Sheri assured her. "In the meantime you need to talk to your parents."

"All right, I'm going. I'll talk to you later."

Sheri nodded, grabbed her things then hurried out with Genie in front of her. Sheri drove to the county courthouse. She was furious. She parked and quickly went inside. It was nearly ten o'clock. That meant all court proceedings had already started for the day. She knew her uncle's docket was probably full, so she hoped to catch him between cases. She walked down the large, open corridors leading to the main courtrooms. She stopped at the last door, opened it and quietly stepped inside.

The courtroom was small with a low ceiling and bright fluorescent lighting even though there were two huge windows on one of the walls. It was sparsely decorated with government-issue furniture and dingy off-white walls. Sheri took a seat in the back row and waited patiently for her uncle to issue a ruling in the case before him. She knew the courtroom protocol. Her uncle would call a recess after the case.

The activity in the Virginia circuit courtroom wasn't as dramatic as it seemed when she sometimes watched on television. There were no surprise witnesses and no courtroom drama. Her uncle was seated on the bench with his clerk and a bailiff on either side. Two lawyers were seated at tables facing him, representing the opposing sides. They were all intently listening to the judge's ruling. After her uncle banged his gavel everyone stood and waited for him to leave before filing out. She remained seated, knowing her uncle and his clerk would be busy for a few more minutes.

When the courtroom was nearly cleared, Sheri walked out and headed to her uncle's office. She turned down the hall to the main judges' suites and continued to the last row of offices. When she got to the door of her uncle's chambers she stopped a moment before entering. She knew that what she was about to do was the right thing. She also knew what it would most likely do to Jordan Hamilton. He'd be furious. But he left her no alternative. She looked up at the shiny brass plaque on the wall beside the thick wooden door—Office of the Honorable Judge Halbrook T. Summers. This was it.

She opened the door and saw her aunt, Lynnette Summers, sitting at her desk busy typing on her computer keyboard. "Hi, Aunt Lynnette, are you busy?"

Lynnette stopped work and looked up. "Hey Sheri, no, come on in. Hal is in chambers right now. It's good to see you. What are you up to?"

"I just saw Uncle Hal in court," Sheri said. "It's always amazing to see him sitting up there like that. He's so impressive."

"He's my treasure. What he says goes around here in the office and courtroom as it should be. He's the law. But at home we all know it's a different story." She winked.

Sheri chuckled, knowing it was true. Her aunt Lynnette was definitely the one in charge when they were at home. Halbrook loved and adored her. Lynnette and her uncle had known each other since law school. She was forced to drop out in her third year of law school for financial reasons. They lost touch. But they met again years later when she was a paralegal at a law firm. They were married soon after reuniting. Halbrook was appointed to the bench and Lynnette became his administrative assistant. "So, how've you been? Looks like you're really busy around here."

"I'm fine, and yes, good Lord, what a crazy day we're having already. Your uncle's docket must be eight pages long today. I swear there must be something in the air, because it seems like everybody is suing or trying to sue everybody else. So tell me, how've you been? We haven't seen you around for months."

"I'm hanging in there. The tourist season is pretty much over, so I can relax a bit more."

"How's the museum?" Lynnette asked.

"It's good. Actually the museum is what I wanted to talk to Uncle Hal about. Do you think he could spare a little time?"

Lynnette nodded, "Oh, sure, just give him a few minutes. He's on the phone right now and his clerks are in chambers. They should be out soon."

Just as she said that the phone rang. Lynnette excused herself and answered. Sheri stepped away and started looking around the outer office. She remembered this place so well. This had been her favorite hangout after school. The bookshelves were always her favorite. They were lined with law books, awards, plaques and antique jars filled with candy, her aunt's one professed weakness. But the certificates and diplomas didn't belong to Halbrook, they belonged to Lynnette. A few minutes later Lynnette hung up and turned her attention back to their conversation. "So what were we saying?"

"Aunt Lynnette, did you ever want to go back and get your law degree? You could have had a brilliant career instead of getting married."

She paused and smiled. "I love the law, I always have. And yes, I think I would have been a brilliant attorney, too. But being a wife and mother changed my life in ways you'd never believe. I could have done both to some degree, but it was my choice to be a brilliant wife and mom."

"Do you think you lost yourself in your choice?"

"What do you mean? If I lost and gave up being me to be Mrs. Somebody and Mom Somebody?" she asked.

Sheri nodded.

"No, not at all. Marriage, the right marriage, to the right person doesn't erase who you are, it enhances it. I've never felt invisible to Halbrook or the kids. It was never a sacrifice to me. I'm still me."

"And now that everybody's grown up, any regrets?"

"No. I love my life now more than ever, just as it is. Being a wife and mother didn't deprive me, it enriched me," she said as she looked at her niece oddly. "Why do you ask? Are you thinking about taking that step, marriage?"

"I was just wondering."

"You know it was Mamma Lou and your grandmother Camille who got me and your uncle back together again."

"Really? I didn't know that."

"Oh, yes, when those two ladies put their heads together there's magic and, most importantly, there's love." Lynnette noticed the light went off on her phone console. A few minutes later the door opened and her uncle's two clerks walked out. "Sheri, it looks like he just got off the telephone. Why don't you go ahead in," Lynnette said.

Sheri headed down the short hall to her uncle's private chambers. She knocked twice softly and then opened the door. She peeked in before going all the way inside. His office was exactly like you'd expect a judge's office to look like. His black robe was on a hanger beside his desk. There was an American Flag, a Virginia flag, a back wall of bookshelves, a conference table and four chairs and a seating area. Her uncle was standing at the wall-length bookshelf with several books in his hand.

He looked so much like her father, particularly when he was serious like now. After her dad died it was her uncle Hal who became the father figure in her and her brothers' lives. He was always a lifesaver and a miracle worker. She just hoped her uncle had one more miracle left for her. Sheri knocked again. He turned, looked up and smiled. "Uncle Hal, it's me, hi," she said.

He smiled, too. "Hey, don't just stand in the doorway like that. Come in, come in. Get over here and give your favorite uncle a hug." Sheri went in and closed the door behind her. As she walked over, he met her halfway. They hugged warmly. "So, how've you been?" he asked.

"I've been good, and you?"

"Righting the ills of the world," he said jokingly. "Now I haven't seen you in a few months, everything okay?"

"I know I haven't been around in a while. I've been crazy busy at the museum, but now that it's almost off-season, I can get out a lot more and visit. So, I was in the area and thought I'd stop by."

He chuckled again. "Okay, even the worst offender wouldn't give me a lousy line like that." They laughed. "Okay, now tell me what *really* brings you here this morning?"

Sheri took a deep breath and released it slowly. "I hate how you see right through me."

"You're my niece, I'm supposed to. Now come have a seat and tell what's going on," he said, placing the books on the credenza behind his desk. He turned and motioned for her to have a seat.

"I have a problem and I'm hoping maybe you can help."

"What can I do for you?" he asked, sitting down behind his big wooden desk.

"I need a court order."

He looked at her oddly. "An injunction, that's pretty serious. Why do you think you need a court order?" he asked.

"There's a construction company called Hamilton Development…"

"Yes, I know of them. They're building a resort complex out at Crescent Point. I understand it's going to be nice. I'm looking forward to seeing it complete. What about them?"

"My assistant at the museum was sent photos of items that led me to believe there might be something of value on the property. I need time to check it out, maybe even excavate."

"What exactly do you mean something of value on the property? What's out there?"

"I don't know for sure, but I believe it might be the wreckage of a ship."

He looked at her without expression.

"I think it might be the *Crescent*."

"The *Crescent*, wow, that *would* be something of value," he said, then paused, knowing her long-felt interest in the *Crescent*. "Okay, where are these items that were found?"

"I don't know exactly. I believe the company does and is withholding information."

"It's their property."

"I know that, but can't something be done? If they trash them or destroy them everything will be lost."

"So you're telling me this person has these items in his possession. Items that don't belong to him and that he doesn't intend to hand them over to you. Do you have proof these items might indeed be thrown away or destroyed or that they are what you think?"

"No, but they have no idea what they are."

"Apparently, neither do you," he said.

"I need to see them and do research. I can't do that if the site is destroyed and it's covered over to make a cement parking lot. I just need them to shut down for a few days, maybe a week at the most."

He shook his head. "All passions aside, Sheri, I understand and sympathize with your dilemma. But it's not for you to impose that type of demand. You have no viable proof."

"That's because it's a catch-22. I can't get the proof if it no longer exists. If he covers that hole or destroys it in any way we would have possibly lost one of the most valuable finds this century."

He shook his head. "There's nothing I can do," said her uncle.

"Okay, what if I go there this evening and get…"

He held his hand up to stop her and shook his head vigorously. "No, the law is the law and you're dancing very close to criminal intent. I can't have that."

"Then how else am I supposed to save the site?"

"Have you tried talking to Mr. Hamilton?"

"Yes."

"No, Sheri, I mean really talking to him? Remember you're my niece. I know your temper and I know how adamant you can be when it comes to what you believe is right, particularly when it pertains to the museum."

"I thought he understood, but apparently he lied and I was wrong. He knew about the anchor and chest and never said a word to me."

"Perhaps you just need a third party's intercession."

"That's why I'm here. I want you to order an injunction."

"There's no probable cause," he told her.

"A week, that's all I need," she pleaded.

"If you had any kind of proof then maybe I could—"

"Scholars have always ascertained that the *Crescent* made it back to Africa. It didn't. It broke up on the reef at Crescent Point. There's no real physical proof and if Jordan gets his way there never will be. I have a diary that belonged to Anne Louise Black. Her tombstone is in the Shanty cemetery. She writes that the boat sank and she and her husband saw the lighthouse and swam ashore. There was only one lighthouse on the island and it was built during the Revolutionary War. It's near the point." She handed him the diary. "This is all the proof I have. Everything else will probably be a parking lot by the end of the week."

Hal smiled and shook his head. "My dear, you missed your calling. You should have gone into law. So you're basically disputing the official findings," he said.

"Yes," she said.

"And what will proving this do?" he added

"Maybe put a few souls to rest. Maybe solve a century-and-a-half-old puzzle, maybe correct historical accuracy and change history or maybe nothing at all," Sheri replied.

Halbrook looked at the tattered diary. After a while he sighed heavily. "It's pretty thin. Granted, there are several precedents that warrant an emergency injunction and perhaps in this case it would give all parties involved enough time to work this out amicably," he said to her pointedly. "Do you understand what I'm saying to you?"

She agreed reluctantly. "Yes, I need to work this through outside of the legal system."

"Exactly, I'm gonna process a seventy-two-hour protective order. That's three days to do what you need to do." He grabbed his phone and called Lynnette and then the sheriff's office. He made the necessary arrangements. The paperwork would be delivered to the sheriff's office immediately, and the actual petition would be served first thing in the morning. The whole procedure took about twenty minutes. When he was done he addressed Sheri. "Okay, you have your emergency injunction for the Hamilton Development building site at Crescent Point."

"Thank you, Uncle Hal."

"Don't thank me yet. It's thin and I'm sure his attorneys will be all over this first thing tomorrow morning. But for right now you have three days to do what you have to do. Make the best of them."

"I understand. I will," she said, standing to leave.

"I hope so," he said. Then he saw her heading for the office door. "Whoa, hold on a minute, young lady. This meeting isn't over. A favor such as this is going to come with a few contingency requirements attached." She stopped walking and turned back around.

"What kind of contingency requirements?" she asked cautiously, knowing her uncle's flair for the theatric.

He smiled. "First, I want you to contact Mr. Hamilton as soon as possible and get this worked out."

Her jaw dropped. "Uncle Hal, he won't listen, I know it. I tried."

"Then try harder. I would think that if you have time to come talk to me about getting a protective order, than you have time to talk to him about making this work."

She paused a moment, seeing he wasn't going to let her off that easily. "Okay, I will."

"Good, that's what I want to hear. Are you headed home now?" he asked.

"No, I need to get back to the museum. I have a lot of work to do, tons of research to dig out, and three days to make this work."

"Okay, I'll see you later."

"See you later, Uncle Hal." Sheri smiled as she left the office. She was relieved. She'd done it. The petition would be delivered tomorrow. She intended to be at the site getting all the samples and information she needed soon after. But right now she needed to get back to the museum and prepare. She had arrangements to plan and phone calls to make. She also needed to gather more information on the *Crescent*. She had three days to make this work.

The rest of Jordan's day was just as insane. They had people trying to sneak in all day. From sunup to sundown they came in droves. They tried to slip over the fence, dig under, cut through. Some dressed like construction workers to sneak in, and still others tried to bribe their way beyond the gate. Nothing got done. It was madness. They came on foot, by car, by bike and even by boat. Jordan spent the day rebuffing reports and talking to his brothers and Kenneth while reassuring the workers that everything would get back to normal soon.

Nolan called to offer his full cooperation, for a perk of course. Jamie's father called, referring to the actions of his twenty-two-year-old son as a kid's prank. He threatened to sue since pictures of his son crying like a baby, trapped in a hole and covered with mud, surfaced everywhere and he looked like a fool. There was also a video circulating on YouTube. It was a three-ring circus complete with clowns and jokers.

Later, he called Sheri to hear a voice of sanity, but she never picked up. He left a message and realized she hadn't returned any of his calls all day. His heart told him something was wrong, but he dismissed it. After all, he'd just spent the weekend with the woman he loved, how could anything possibly be wrong?

He was very wrong.

Chapter 20

Tuesday morning the sun tipped over the horizon. The day promised to be bright and sunny. At dawn two sheriff's cars pulled back into the parking lot. The deputies got out and served the paperwork. Five minutes later the Hamilton Development Corporation site was shut down by order of the Honorable Judge Halbrook T. Summers.

All hell broke loose soon after. The security guards on duty called Cleveland. He picked up the phone and started a tsunami of phone calls. Jordan got the call. His brothers got the call. Kenneth got the call. Fifty men and woman were locked out and all work came to a screeching halt. It was all over the local news by seven o'clock that morning.

Jordan went to the site, grabbed the paperwork and headed to the airport. The private plane arrived on time. It coasted down the runway, turned and stopped. The hatch opened and three men stepped up to depart. Jordan walked across the tarmac to meet them. Darius was the first one off the plane. "Hey, how you doing?" he said sternly, shaking his hand and hugging. "You look good." Although he resembled Jordan, there was still an air of authority and privileged power surrounding him.

Darius was the older brother by two years. A very successful stockbroker with a portfolio that would put most hedge funds to shame. He was the more serious and levelheaded of the three. It was his idea they all take over their father's construction business. And due to his savvy business know-how, they had yet to make a misstep.

Julian stepped down next. "Bro, no worries, we got this. Treasure, I like it, nice PR save." They shook hands and hugged. Julian was the middle brother and the only one married. He'd been a doctor before giving up his practice to join Hamilton Development. He always said it was the best decision he ever made. His specialty was negotiations. His deals were brilliant. He could psyche out the competition and potential client using only his charm and guile.

The last off the plane was Kenneth Fields. He was their brother in every way except blood. A few months ago the Hamiltons even added his name to the board of directors. He was now part of the corporation. "Jordan, my man," he said, seeming happy to be on the offensive. "Let's do this." He was a shark in the courtroom and had contacts all the way to the Supreme Court and beyond. Jordan handed him the court order. He started reading immediately.

Jordan followed them to the car. He hoped Crescent Island was ready to contend with Hamilton Development, but he doubted it. He got in and drove into town.

"Game plan, we keep the artifacts on site," Darius said. "Is Cleveland still shooing away reporters and trespassers?"

"No, I have him guarding the two items we pulled out the other night. They're already off-site," Jordan said.

"Good."

"Where are they?" Julian asked.

"No, we don't need to know at this point," Kenneth interjected then continued texting. "Okay, we have an appointment with Judge Halbrook T. Summers in thirty minutes."

"Last name, Summers?" Jordan said.

"Yeah, he signed the order. Do you know him?"

"No, but I might know his relative, Sheri Summers, the woman from the video. Art museum, the woman I told you about."

"Okay, that might be a problem," Kenneth said.

"Yep, it's personal," Julian said. Kenneth nodded.

"We need a new game plan," Darius said.

"What's the background story with this ship?" Julian asked.

Jordan told them what he learned about the *Crescent* and its importance to the island. "Proving its existence here after all these years could change the history books. It's widely assumed the ship made it back to Africa. If it didn't, there will be a lot of people interested in knowing that."

"Excellent, so our role in this brings very positive publicity and a hell of a Hamilton Development historical footnote."

"Okay, so the plan is to make it work with Sheri Summers."

They all nodded. Jordan didn't. He was outvoted, so it didn't matter, but still they each looked at him. "Can you make this work, Jordan? You're the key," Darius asked. He nodded.

"One more thing, are we talking about remains? That could change everything." They all went silent.

"I don't think so," Jordan finally said. "Sheri mentioned a woman who swam to shore and how everyone was saved, but the ship and her belongings were lost."

"We need confirmation. Get a team out here and go through every square inch of the site. We need whatever's there properly documented."

Jordan parked beside the Rantone Building and turned the engine off. They got out of the car and walked to the front door. "So what are you going to do?" Julian asked.

Jordan looked at him, confused. Darius and Kenneth were staring at him, too. "About what?" he asked.

"About Sheri," Julian said.

"I don't understand," Jordan said.

"Told you he'd say that," Darius said, holding his hand out.

Julian groaned and placed a ten-dollar bill in Darius's hand. "Do you love her?" Darius asked.

"No," he lied. Julian laughed and received the money back. "Yes," he said, confessing. Darius took the wager back still laughing.

"Did you ask her to marry you yet?" Kenneth asked.

"Yes," Jordan said. Julian and Darius groaned and each pulled a hundred-dollar bill out of their pocket and handed it to Kenneth. He chuckled as they entered the building, "Okay, let's do this."

Sheri walked into the museum already feeling exhausted. Her plan was all set to go. She had planned on Genie helping out. But thanks to Jamie blaming her, she had a lot of questions to answer in the next few days. Several of her Smithsonian colleagues, including forensics and pathology archaeologists, would be coming in the following day to fully examine the site for human remains and other anomalies. Right now she needed to grab her samples kit, camera and backpack and get out there to begin preparations as soon as possible.

"Hey, Sheri, did you hear what happened up at the Hamilton construction site this morning?"

"Yeah, I know," she said, hurrying to her office.

"A shame, huh, all those people out of a job. That's sad, especially in this economy."

She stopped and backtracked. "Wait, what do you mean?"

"Didn't you hear? They closed the site this morning?"

"What, no, they closed down the secondary site."

"Nah, I don't know anything about a secondary site. I know my brothers work out there and they got the day off. But hey, the Hamiltons are all right with me. It's gonna be considered paid leave, plus bonus."

"Oh, no." Her heart dropped instantly. She ran up the steps, dialing at the same time. She got to her office and scrambled to her desk. The phone on the other end picked up. "Hi, Aunt Lynnette, is Uncle Hal available?"

"I'm sorry, dear, he's in a closed-door meeting right now. You sound rushed—are you okay?"

"No, Aunt Lynnette, I'm not. I made a mistake when I was talking to Uncle Hal yesterday. I didn't specify that I only meant the secondary site might have remnants of the *Crescent,* not the whole construction site. All those people didn't have to be out of work today."

"Oh, dear, that *is* a problem."

"I'm so sorry. Is Uncle Hal in major trouble?"

"Actually he's meeting with the Hamilton Development representatives in about half an hour. Hal's in with Nolan and another member of the board of supervisors right now. Apparently his son caused a bit of trouble on the site and daddy can't get him out of it this time."

"I know Jordan's furious. He and his brothers are gonna want Uncle Hal's head."

She chuckled. "Sweetheart, your uncle's a sitting judge. He can take care of himself and his head. He'll make sure everything will be fine."

"I hope so."

"Trust me. I'll work it from this end and text you when we're all straight, okay?"

"Thank you, Aunt Lynnette."

"No worries. Let me get started here. I'm sure it will be cleared up within the next few hours."

As soon as she hung up, her phone rang. It was her mother. "Mom, I know, I know. It was a mistake. I'll call you back. My other line is ringing.... Sheri Summers."

"Ms. Summers, I'm calling from the *Crescent Online Dispatch.* Can you tell me anything about the discovery up at Crescent Point?"

"What?"

"The site was closed this morning because valuable artifacts were found on the site. If you could give me a quote for this afternoon's internet post that would be great. About how much is it worth exactly?"

"Um, I'm sorry, no comment." She hung up and stared at the phone. "Everyone thinks there's some kind of treasure," she muttered.

"Yes, they do." Sheri looked up to see Jordan standing in the doorway. "That's what I told them. You see, how could I tell them the truth? That the woman I love shut the site down and put more than fifty men and woman out of work to hurt me and to make a point. And of course to dig up a few scattered relics, most of which are sitting in a box in your living room. This is for you." He handed her the envelope Cleveland had given him.

She took it then remembered the box he had brought over Friday night. She never looked inside. "Jordan, no, it was a mistake."

"What part? Going to the judge, spending the weekend with me or pretending to love me? Or was it having your assistant and her boyfriend repeatedly break into the site to dig through dirt with a flashlight and destroy property while you distracted me? Do you have any idea how dangerous that was? Anything could have happened to them out there and it would have been our fault."

"No, it's not like that. I didn't…" Her phone rang again. She grabbed it, hitting the intercom button.

"Sheri, there's a problem down on the loading dock."

"Okay, I'll be right there."

"No, it's an emergency. You need to come now."

"I'm on my way." As soon as she hung up, her phone rang again. She let the call go to voice mail then turned to continue her conversation. "Jordan…" He was gone.

She hurried into the hall. He was nowhere in sight. She grabbed her cell and ran downstairs to the front desk. "Where's the man who came to see me?" she asked breathlessly.

"He just left."

She put the envelope on the desk and ran out front, in time to see Jordan's truck drive away She went back inside. "Sheri, they need you out back right now. Don't forget your phone." She nodded woefully. He'd just walked out. She headed to the loading dock. As soon as she stepped out onto the platform she saw that a large chunk of wall had fallen from the side of the building. She stared at the rubble on the ground. This was her life. She shook her head, reminded security to take pictures for their report and went back to her desk. She called the maintenance crew then listened to a half-dozen messages she had just missed. Four were from newspapers, one from a television station and one from her supervisor. She pressed the button for speaker.

"Sheri, it's Jack. What the hell is going on there? The Hamilton Development attorney called my bosses' bosses and they're all over me. They also received calls from a member of the board and the chair of the Smithsonian. I'm on my way. What treasure? We need to talk."

She sat down and shook her head. It was all wrong. Hopefully her aunt and uncle could fix things. There was no sense in going to the work site. She couldn't get in. The whole place had been shut down. She turned on her computer and tried to work, but it was no use. She just stared at the monitor.

"Knock, knock."

She looked up seeing Mamma Lou and her grandmother Camille in the doorway. They were exactly who she needed to see. "Hi, come in please. Have a seat." She got up and kissed each woman as she sat down. "I guess you heard. It was my fault. I was so obsessed with the idea that Jordan had destroyed precious artifacts that I didn't clarify which site I meant when I talked to Uncle Hal."

"That's easily resolved," Louise said.

"Sheri," her grandmother began. "History is one thing. Your future is another. Don't spend so much time looking back that you can't see what's right in front of you."

"Yes, love," Louise said.

The word instantly pierced her heart. He had said it and she didn't hear it until now. *"How could I tell them the truth. That the woman I love..."* He had said it again and she didn't even hear him. "He loves me," she whispered. Camille and Louise nodded in unison. "He loves me and I love him."

"Go to him, tell him."

"How can I, after everything that's happened?"

"This is when he needs to know," Camille said. "Go, now."

Sheri grabbed her backpack and cell phone as Louise and Camille stood up. They walked to the elevators talking about the party and the upcoming Thanksgiving holiday. Louise planned a huge family meal and of course everyone was expected to come.

The security guard looked up as they approached. "Sheri, I was just about to call you. You have a delivery to sign for."

"A delivery? I'm not expecting anything today."

"It's from Gates Antiques," he said. She looked confused. There was no reason Tony would be sending anything to her.

"Goodbye, dear," Louise said.

Sheri hugged and kissed them again. "Thank you so much for coming by to see me. I'll call you later." She watched them leave then turned in the opposite direction, and headed to the loading dock again. There was a Gates truck open and two large crates waiting. "Where's the paperwork on this delivery?" The security guard pointed to the man standing beside the truck. Sheri recognized him instantly. "Cleveland," she said. He nodded. "What is this?"

"Jordan wanted it delivered to you."

"The anchor and chest," she said. He handed her the paperwork. She signed off on it and had the men move the crates into the museum storage area. "Thank you." Sheri headed back to the front just as Jack McDonald walked in. "Jack, I just got your message. I'm on my way out."

"This won't take long," he said firmly. "Your office."

"Sure." They went back to her office. She sat at her desk as Jack took a seat across from her.

"Before we discuss what's going on at the Hamilton site there's something you should know. The Crescent Island Museum will no longer be funded. I'm sorry. The exhibits will be returned to their original museums or distributed to other museums. The doors will officially close next month."

She was stunned. "What? I don't understand."

"Sheri, we can't keep funding this building and we can't afford to renovate. We tried having it designated as a historical site and we failed. We have no choice, we have to move on. We very recently received an offer to purchase this building."

"You're selling the building, too?"

"Yes. The Hamilton Development Corporation has made a very—"

"The Hamilton Development Corporation? They bought it?"

"Well, not quite. We're very early in negotiations, but I don't see any reason why it shouldn't go through."

"What are they going to do with it?" she asked nervously.

Jack shrugged. "Tear it down, I assume. What else?"

"When did they make the offer?"

"Officially, yesterday," he said.

"Yesterday?" she repeated, shaking her head. "I can't believe it."

"Sheri, the closing is essentially a done deal. It's been in the works for the past twelve months. As we discussed earlier, I'd like you to return to the Smithsonian. Your expertise is invaluable there. Now, as for this business out at the site, our official response is *no comment*. There is no treasure or maps or valuables or any other nonsense."

"Jack, I'd like to start at the museum immediately, right now, today."

"Ah, I'm not sure that's possible. Staying here would be best for all involved."

"I can't."

"Sheri, I realize this is difficult. This is your hometown, right? I think you supervising the closing of the museum instead of a stranger would ease the transition for local residents. They'll see you're okay with it and…"

"No."

"Sheri, I'm afraid leaving today is impossible. There's a press conference scheduled and I'd like you there with us."

She didn't respond. She was numb. She hadn't seen any of this coming. He had used her, distracted her to get another building. Her phone beeped. She looked at the message from her aunt.

The order was rescinded—it was then reissued stipulating the secondary site only—effective Wednesday a.m. Now go get your treasure!

She functioned on autopilot the rest of the day. Thankfully it had calmed down considerably from the craziness earlier. She left early. There was nothing more to do. On the way out the guard handed her the envelope she had left at the desk earlier. She took it and kept going.

She drove home and as soon as she stepped

through the door she saw the box Jordan mentioned. She walked over, dropped her purse and the envelope and opened the box. It was what she'd expected. He had given her the artifacts Friday night and she didn't even see them. She collapsed back on the sofa and grabbed the envelope he gave her earlier. She opened it and pulled out the tattered book. She sat up. She knew that book. She knew this writing. She'd read the one in the glass case a dozen times before. But this wasn't it. This was something new.

She very carefully opened the book to the first page. She smiled and gasped at the same time. Her heart beat faster as she read the first sentence. "Our son, Nicholas, was born…"

Sheri didn't stop until she'd read the whole thing. Afterward she got up and went to her mother's house. Both she and her grandmother were still up. They were in the kitchen drinking tea. Sheri walked in, smiling. Lois and Camille looked up. "Sheri, what brings you out this late?"

"Anne Louise Black was Nicholas's mother. She died giving birth to her second child."

"What?"

Camille clapped her hands. "Yes, yes, I knew it. I knew it. It all makes sense."

"What do you mean? How do you know?" Lois said.

"It's all in here, Anne's second diary. Jordan

gave it to me." Sheri sat down and started reading the diary to her mother and grandmother. It told of Anne's struggles and triumphs. She wrote detailed stories about her new husband and her young son, Nicholas, and her new life on Crescent Island, named after the ship that sank bringing them. The last entry talked about the coming birth of her second child. Lois and Camille barely breathed while Sheri read from the book a second time.

"My grandmother once told me a story about her mother. I never remembered her name. She was born as her mother died. It was Anne."

"I guess that's why she always seemed so special to me. She's my ancestor."

Camille nodded. "She came looking for a new life, for change. She found love."

"She didn't live long."

"She lived long enough. She had two children and now she has us, all of us. Her struggles made everything possible."

"Where did Jordan get it?" Lois asked Sheri.

"I don't know. We aren't exactly together. I was the one who got Uncle Hal to close the site, but it was a mistake. Then I found out that he and his brothers bought the museum building."

"Well, that's a relief," Camille said.

"Grandma, Nicholas built that building. It's history."

"It's also time to make it new, to change it."

"Did you talk to Jordan and tell him?" Lois asked.

"You love him," Camille said, after holding her hand.

"Yes. But I thought you couldn't see people close to you."

"Sweetheart, it doesn't take a clairvoyant to see how you feel about each other. He loves you and you love him. Seeing you dance out on the patio was all I needed. Now, I need sleep and so do you, because you have a lot of fixing to do tomorrow."

Chapter 21

The Wednesday evening press conference went off without a hitch, assuring that the opening of Hamilton Resort Complex would be a huge success. Nolan took full credit for everything as usual and was probably having a plaque made congratulating himself. Jack poked his chest out as he gave business cards to anyone and everyone whether they wanted one or not. Mamma Lou and Camille came and graciously sat up front with several other notaries. Colonel Wheeler was there, too, but he knew so many people he was never in one place for long.

The statements by Darius Hamilton were succinct. "We are pleased to report all the items found on this site have been collected and delivered to the Crescent Island Museum for full analysis. The history of the *Crescent* ship is available at the museum and on the museum's website. We have uncovered a number of significant artifacts including the *Crescent*'s bell, the ship's anchor and a chest whose contents will be opened by museum officials. We are cooperating fully and received word this afternoon that there are no other artifacts on the property."

Jack took the podium next, and then Nolan and finally Kenneth Fields handled all the questions. Afterward there was a small reception. Lois planned, set up and catered the event. She thought of everything including Hamilton hard hats as souvenirs. Everyone smiled and posed for photos, but no one knew the real toll this took. Sheri hung back letting Jack take his bows. When questions about the museum were asked, he shuffled and dodged as always, saying everything and nothing. No one could parse that it was all over.

After the press conference and reception, Darius and Julian took a group of reporters over to tour the main structure. Sheri saw Jordan go into the trailer. She followed. She had to confront him. He had accused her of knowing about Genie and Jamie. Now it was her turn to clear the air. She knocked and went inside. Jordan was standing at his drafting table staring down at one of his renderings. She walked over. Her anger had long since subsided.

She was calm. All she felt now was heartache at being taken advantage of.

He looked up as she approached. "You accused me of using you. I had no idea what Genie and her boyfriend were up to. I never lied to you. I only wanted you to see the real Crescent Island."

"I know. I'm sorry. I was wrong."

"In the meantime you were making plans to buy my museum."

"We didn't buy the museum. We made an offer to buy the building. There's a difference."

She shook her head. "It's the same thing. The building is the history."

"No, it's not. It's a structure that falls down around you that has major electrical problems and hasn't been maintained for years. It has no reliable heating and air-conditioning system. And the foundation is so weak the building is two seconds from collapsing. That means everyone and everything in it is in immediate danger. It should be condemned, and I have no idea why it hasn't been."

Sheri thought about the crumbling bricks she saw beside the loading dock the day before. "You don't know that for sure."

"I know," he stated definitively.

She took a deep breath and turned away as tears welled in her eyes. She knew he was right. Holding on to something when she knew in her heart she needed to let go wasn't easy. But she had to and that included him. She nodded. "Goodbye, Jordan."

"Sheri, I'm doing this for you," he said softly.

She whipped around. "By taking everything away from me? By changing my life, by closing the museum?"

"By giving you everything you love," he said.

She shook her head as the tears fell. "Don't talk to me about love. You don't know anything about love. I gave you my love and you threw it back in my face."

She turned to leave again. He grabbed her arms and pulled her back. He was breathing hard and there was pain and anguish in his eyes. "I…" he began, then stopped and took a deep breath and started again. "I love you and I would never, ever hurt you. I did this for you. This—" he reached back and grabbed the paper on his desk and held it out for her "—is for you."

She looked down at what he'd been working on. She saw it, but then wasn't sure. Then it was clear. It was Nicholas's building, but better. Tears erupted. He was saving her. "Jordan…"

He grabbed her in his arms and held her tight. "I love you. I love you."

"I love you, too."

Sheri closed her eyes, feeling a happiness she had never experienced but always hoped to find. "I can't believe this is happening. It's so fast."

"No, it's just right. It's our time. Now, if I remember correctly, I asked you a question. Will you marry me?"

"Yes, I will," she said happily.

He kissed and hugged her again.

"Wait, how are we going to do this? I don't even know where you really live. Do you have a house or a farm or an apartment or a…"

He laughed. "We will live anywhere you want."

"While the museum is being renovated, I'm being transferred to D.C."

"Perfect. I have a house just outside the city."

"You know Mamma Lou is going to be incorrigible after this."

"Yeah, I know, but she was right."

Sheri nodded. "Yes, she was. You are perfect for me."

"Are you ready to tell everybody?" he asked.

She nodded. He took her hand and they walked to the door of the trailer. He kissed her once more and opened the door. There was a loud resounding cheer. They turned to see their family and friends applauding. "I think they already know."

Later, while Jordan met with his brothers, Nolan and Jack, Sheri went back to the museum and worked late. She walked around the exhibits as if taking one last look. There were two centuries' worth of history here. Less than half the people on the island had ever crossed the museum threshold.

Maybe Jordan was right. Change was coming and history was only for books. But she knew it was still important and she'd still fight to make sure it was remembered.

She touched the glass case, seeing the first artifact Nicholas had found on the beach. Old, tattered and nearly disintegrating, it was her favorite piece. She smiled as she thought of the world it came from. Then, hearing footsteps, she looked up.

"Sheri," the night guard said, "you have a visitor."

Jordan walked over to her. "You ready to go home?" he asked.

She nodded then looked around again. In one month everything would be gone. She looked back at the glass case.

"Anne's diary," he said.

She nodded again. "The writing is just childlike script, but it says so much. It epitomized everything here. There's a life and a story in this and every relic and artifact in this building. They're not just things—they belonged to people, people who lived and danced and sang and loved and died."

"And you will continue to collect memories and tell their histories just like Camille does, but in a different way. And just like Nicholas did all those years ago. But this time in a building that will be safe and modern and worthy of everything here. We just have to make sure that in another hundred years our great-great-granddaughter lets change come a bit more easily than her ancestor, Sheri Summers Hamilton."

"What? I don't understand. What are you talking about?"

"Hamilton Development has officially offered to rebuild the Crescent Island Museum," he said. Sheri's jaw dropped. "Everyone loved the design. We need to take the next step."

She threw her arms around him and squealed. "Thank you, thank you, thank you. I love you."

"I love you, too."

"And yes, I'll make a notation in the cornerstone—please rebuild every hundred years. And maybe I'll put my diary inside, as well." He laughed. "Wait, I know exactly where I want to put everything. The anchor will be near the entrance right by the doorway."

"And the treasure chest?" he asked.

"Anne's beloved belongings will be right in the middle. She will be the centerpiece of the exhibit."

"Just as you are the centerpiece of my life," he said, nuzzling her close. "Mmm, this is love," he said. "This is what I never thought I'd feel. You're the love I've been waiting for all my life." He took her hand and kissed it. As he did he slipped a stunning emerald ring encircled with diamond baguettes on her finger. "For you," he whispered.

Sheri gasped, speechless. In all her dreams and

fantasies she never ever thought this moment could come true. "Jordan, it's beautiful. I've never seen anything like. It's…" She turned and wrapped her arms around his body. "Yes, yes, forever and ever, yes."

"Come on, let's get out of here and start making our own history."

Epilogue

Thanksgiving Day was a time to celebrate family and friends and when Louise Gates celebrated, it was a gala event. Everyone came and had an incredible time. After dinner Jordan and Sheri walked down the pathway and across the garden bridge to the other side of the pond. Jordan had built a gazebo for Mamma Lou months ago. Sheri stood at the railing and looked out over the beautiful landscape. "Happy?" he asked, standing behind his wife.

"I'm overjoyed."

"Then why do you look so despondent?"

"I'm gonna miss this place so much," she said.

"Yeah, me, too. But it's not like we're never coming back. I have a feeling we're gonna be coming back here a lot."

She nodded slowly. "I hope so," she said.

"We will, our family is here," he assured her. "And speaking of family, you know our wedding at the courthouse was wonderful, but I think we're gonna have to do it again."

"Again? Why?" she asked.

"I think my new grandmother deserves something a bit more to celebrate."

"You're probably right about that. I guess I'll have to start planning a wedding. I can't believe everything has changed so much. This isn't how I saw this happening."

"You saw it?" he asked.

She nodded. "I thought I did. Actually I thought I had my grandma Camille's gift of seeing. But I never saw this."

"Camille told me that love changes everything. That's why she can't read her family members or those close to her."

Sheri turned and smiled up at her husband. "Did you know that this is my favorite place to be in the whole world?" she said.

"Gates Manor or Crescent Island?" he asked.

"No, here in your arms," she said.

He smiled and nodded.

"There's no place I'll ever feel more loved."

"This is forever," he whispered in her ear.

She nodded with tears in her eyes. "Yes, forever."

Hearing the strain in her voice, Jordan turned her around and looked into her eyes. "What's wrong?" he asked, concerned.

She shook her head. "Nothing, I'm fine. I'm more than fine. I'm so very happy. I never thought I could feel so much joy." She reached up and tenderly touched the smoothness of his face. "I am happier than I ever thought I'd be."

"Me, too," Jordan said. He leaned down and kissed her passionately. An unexpected movement in the garden got their attention. Mamma Lou and Colonel Wheeler walked hand in hand across the brightly lit bridge heading back toward the manor. The love that surrounded them shone through.

"Can you see us at that age walking hand in hand, still so much in love with each other?"

"Yes, I can see it," Jordan said, pulling Sheri into his arms. He leaned down and kissed her tenderly. "This is only the beginning of our history."

* * * * *

Three classic stories
from three beloved voices in romance.

USA TODAY Bestselling Author
KAYLA PERRIN

&

Essence Bestselling Authors
DONNA HILL
ADRIANNE BYRD

The holiday season can bring
unexpected good fortune.
In this sexy short-story
collection, three women's
holiday fantasies are fulfilled
in the most unconventional
ways....

*Coming the first week of November 2011
wherever books are sold.*

KIMANI PRESS™

www.kimanipress.com

KPHF4541111

The exciting
conclusion to the
Hopewell General
miniseries…

CASE OF DESIRE

HOPEWELL GENERAL

Essence
Bestselling Author

JACQUELIN
THOMAS

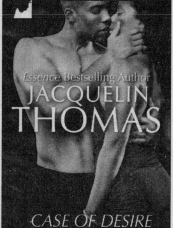

KIMANI ROMANCE

Essence Bestselling Author
JACQUELIN
THOMAS

CASE OF DESIRE
HOPEWELL GENERAL

Successful attorney Maxwell Wade has never lost a case. Hired
by Hopewell General to settle a potentially explosive lawsuit, the
freewheeling bachelor plans to continue his winning streak by
getting Camille Hunter into bed. But she doesn't plan to be just
another notch in his belt. Until Max stuns her with a passionate
declaration and makes his case…for love!

HOPEWELL GENERAL
A PRESCRIPTION FOR PASSION

Coming the first week of November 2011
wherever books are sold.

KIMANI™
ROMANCE

www.kimanipress.com

KPJT2321111

Four wish lists.
Two holiday stories.

The most wonderful
time of the year.

Baby,
Let It
Snow

Beverly
Jenkins

Elaine
Overton

BEVERLY JENKINS
ELAINE OVERTON

KIMANI ROMANCE

Baby, *Let It* Snow

In *I'll Be Home for Christmas* by Beverly Jenkins, a surprise
reunion between two ex-lovers leads to a conflict over a family
business…and an unexpected rekindling of romance.

In *Second Chance Christmas* by Elaine Overton, one couple is
reunited for the holidays…and they discover a season perfect
for forgiving and loving….

Coming the first week of November 2011
wherever books are sold.

KIMANI™
ROMANCE

www.kimanipress.com

KPBJEO2331111

*She's on his
Christmas list—
this time for keeps!*

A *Christmas Affair*

**Essence
Bestselling Author**

Adrianne Byrd

As president of a talent agency, Chloe Banks is a New York City success story. But beneath the facade is a small-town girl whose past is a closely guarded secret. Until Lyfe Alton, her girlhood sweetheart, resurfaces. With Chloe in his arms, can Lyfe turn their sizzling Christmas affair into a season for second chances?

**"Totally hilarious with great characters, a strong plot
and scorching-hot love scenes, this story entertains
from beginning to end."**
—*RT Book Reviews* on *BODY HEAT*

*Coming the first week of November 2011
wherever books are sold.*

www.kimanipress.com

KPAB2341111

They're mixing business with pleasure…and it's off the charts!

Ready for **LOVE**

Favorite author **GWYNETH BOLTON**

Maritza Morales and Terrill Carter are partners in a successful music company. But mixing business with pleasure may be a risky proposition unless he can prove he's the only one for her. A wedding with all the trimmings is what Terrill has in mind, because he's in love…and ready for anything!

It's All About Our Men

Coming the first week of November 2011 wherever books are sold.

www.kimanipress.com

KPGB2351111

REQUEST YOUR FREE BOOKS!

2 FREE NOVELS
PLUS 2 FREE GIFTS!

KIMANI™
ROMANCE

Love's ultimate destination!

YES! Please send me 2 FREE Kimani™ Romance novels and my 2 FREE gifts (gifts are worth about $10). After receiving them, if I don't wish to receive any more books, I can return the shipping statement marked "cancel." If I don't cancel, I will receive 4 brand-new novels every month and be billed just $4.94 per book in the U.S. or $5.49 per book in Canada. That's a saving of at least 21% off the cover price. It's quite a bargain! Shipping and handling is just 50¢ per book in the U.S. and 75¢ per book in Canada.* I understand that accepting the 2 free books and gifts places me under no obligation to buy anything. I can always return a shipment and cancel at any time. Even if I never buy another book, the two free books and gifts are mine to keep forever.

168/368 XDN FEJR

Name	(PLEASE PRINT)	

Address		Apt. #

City	State/Prov.	Zip/Postal Code

Signature (if under 18, a parent or guardian must sign)

Mail to the **Reader Service:**

IN U.S.A.: P.O. Box 1867, Buffalo, NY 14240-1867
IN CANADA: P.O. Box 609, Fort Erie, Ontario L2A 5X3

Not valid for current subscribers to Kimani Romance books.

Want to try two free books from another line?
Call 1-800-873-8635 or visit www.ReaderService.com.

* Terms and prices subject to change without notice. Prices do not include applicable taxes. Sales tax applicable in N.Y. Canadian residents will be charged applicable taxes. Offer not valid in Quebec. This offer is limited to one order per household. All orders subject to credit approval. Credit or debit balances in a customer's account(s) may be offset by any other outstanding balance owed by or to the customer. Please allow 4 to 6 weeks for delivery. Offer available while quantities last.

Your Privacy—The Reader Service is committed to protecting your privacy. Our Privacy Policy is available online at www.ReaderService.com or upon request from the Reader Service.

We make a portion of our mailing list available to reputable third parties that offer products we believe may interest you. If you prefer that we not exchange your name with third parties, or if you wish to clarify or modify your communication preferences, please visit us at www.ReaderService.com/consumerschoice or write to us at Reader Service Preference Service, P.O. Box 9062, Buffalo, NY 14269. Include your complete name and address.

KROM11B

NATIONAL BESTSELLING AUTHOR
ROCHELLE
ALERS

Married to some of Washington, D.C.'s, most influential men, Bethany, Deanna and Marisol are on the guest list at every high-profile political and social event. Beneath the glamour, all three are struggling to hide the voids in their marriages. As their friendship deepens, they help each other decide how far they'll go to fulfill their desires.

Because in passion—as in politics—one mistake can change everything....

C PITAL
WIVES

Pick up your copy on October 25, 2011, wherever books are sold.

KIMANI PRESS™

www.kimanipress.com

KPRACWSP

Get ready to celebrate the holidays with the Steele family....

New York Times and *USA TODAY* bestselling author

BRENDA JACKSON

A STEELE FOR CHRISTMAS

Stacy Carlson has no illusions about love. Can her sexy landlord, Eli Steele, turn their strictly business arrangement into a Christmas filled with pleasure…and lasting love?

Pick up your copy on September 27, 2011, wherever books are sold.

www.kimanipress.com

KPBJASFCSP